The No-Death Option

By Brian K. Ellerby

ISBN#: 978-0-615-86583-6

Table of Contents

Synopsis:

The "No-Death Option" is a fictional work centering on Youssef Aziz. Youssef immigrated to the United States with his mother and father the year after Gulf War I to escape persecution from Saddam Hussein for helping the Americans. Youssef has an American education, but unknown to his family and close associates, Youssef maintains close ties with one of the radical Islamic factions in his home country of Iraq. Like a dormant virus in the human body awaiting the right conditions to awaken, so too has Youssef's and his plans lain dormant in America.

Then events at his job cause him to implement his plan of attack on an unsuspecting America. His actions have serious though not deadly effects on Americans but if not stopped would kill their great American engine of consumption, the Economy. The Death of the Economy would result in the death of America without killing its people. The No-Death Option takes current events occurring in our country and tells a gripping story of what could happen if terrorists ever figure out what truly makes America

work.

The "No-Death" Option

The No-Death Option is dedicated to the memory of my loving mother, Ruth Elizabeth (Peguese) Ellerby – June 19, 1930, as the sun rose on a bright blue sky – April 10, 1998, 1:30 a.m., as the sun was poised to rise yet again, your bright blue sky had turned to a gray smoky haze. Your last decade clouded by Alzheimer's but you were able to see through the haze and knew who I was until the end. Love, your baby boy - Brian.

Foreword

Fear not, death is the ultimate weapon. With fear like a virus as it invades a body, it can spread; however, with the death of the host cell, the virus loses its host and the ability to spread. So it is with death, there is no host to spread the fear. The war between good and evil has been fought for generations. The definition of good and evil is in the mind of the beholder. A person who fights to protect his family's way of life when that way of life is under attack by opposing forces will be called evil or radical by the attacker. This spin on the use of two words consisting of four letters each has long been used by the majority to inoculate the minority against opposing the majority's way. Whether against the

Native American Indian or any other indigenous group, leaders intent on conquering their land knew how to use the spin of good versus evil to achieve their desired endpoint. The same is true in the struggle between the Christian and Muslim religions. Many persons living in the West have been conditioned to fear Islam or to distrust someone from a Muslim country. This is also true of Muslim countries and their cultures. Their leaders have taught them not to trust anyone from the West. Good versus evil. The war of words continues.

The West, rich in political and economic wealth, has continued for centuries to move into areas rich with resources, though not welcoming of Western culture. This results in conflict that until the twenty-first century had been won by the West --- not by its intellectual prowess, but by its economic might. As with the Giant Goliath, this advantage would soon come to an end. Some in the Muslim world, the radicals or as the leaders of the West would have one to believe, the evil doers had discovered, as did David in the Bible, a small pebble delivered in the right manner could bring the giant to its knees. The war between good and evil continues.

Chapter 1 – In the Beginning God Created....

It was an unusually warm, sunny, smog-free day in Los Angeles. Malik and his father walked away from Dodgers' Stadium full of happiness; their home team was headed to the playoffs for the first time in ten years. As they walked the three miles back to their neighborhood, Malik asked, "When can we go to another game?" Malik's father, Abdul al-Kariim, had dreamed for years of being a professional baseball player, but after that fateful day in September 2001 everything changed for him.

Malik was thirteen years old, full of energy and was very inquisitive. Malik asked his questions at a rate as fast as the cars going by on the highway. As he darted along the sidewalk leading away from Dodgers' Stadium, he hit his father with a barrage of questions. He wanted to know how many fans were at the game, how much money was earned by the concessions people, and whether all of the money went to the players. Abdul marveled and laughed to himself about his son's ability to ask so many questions. As he walked, he thought, "May Allah bless my son and, more importantly, my son's teachers."

Abdul replied, "Malik, I am glad you enjoyed the game so much. It may be sometime before we are able to come again." Abdul knew it would be some time given the Dodgers' entry into the playoffs and the resulting cost of the tickets. He was only able to take him to the game today because a friend could not make the game and felt it would be a good outing for Abdul and his young son.

Abdul saw himself in his young son when it came to the game of baseball. Malik, like his father, played left field and was an excellent player. His father was proud of his son on and off the field. Not only was Malik an accomplished baseball player, he was also an excellent student. Malik devoured everything in sight at the stadium, and then even having accomplished this feat, Malik asked his father, "Can we stop by the ice cream shop for ice cream?" Smiling, Abdul replied, "Of course, son, as he too wanted to indulge in this family pastime. As they sat on the parlor's outside patio, they marveled at the beauty of the evening stars now appearing in the aqua blue sky. As Abdul watched his son eat his ice cream, he thought to himself, "How far I have come, yet how far I have to go in order to provide the life style he wanted for his family.

Times like this caused Abdul to reflect on his life. Abdul had worked hard throughout his young life after moving to the United States from Saudi Arabia. His grades in high school and his scores on the college entrance exams allowed him to choose his college. He chose UCLA in order to remain close to his home and family in Englewood, California. Malik broke his father's daydream by asking him, "Why did you stop playing baseball in college?" Malik had asked this question many times before, because his father's trophy case in their small house was full of awards from high school and college. Abdul thought now was the time to tell his son the true story of why he stopped playing baseball. "Son, the United States is a place that does not accept those who are not considered a part of the majority. When the majority is threatened by those in the minority, the majority attempts to limit the minority's ability to improve their status. The United States has for years supported policies to hurt thousands of their countrymen back home in Iraq and fellow Muslims in other countries."

"This blind support led to many in their home country of Saudi Arabia and other Muslim countries to hate the United States. This hate, he told his young son, caused nineteen true believers to develop a plan that was enacted on a date no one would soon forget, September 11, 2001. This attack and the resulting harassment of peaceful Muslims caused many of our countrymen in the United States to question whether we belonged." Abdul told his son, "The administrators, professors, and students at UCLA began silently harassing him and others of the Muslim faith."

Confronted with increasing security screens and scrutiny from his professors and school administrators, Abdul told his son, "I gave up on my dream of becoming a professional baseball player." Abdul thought to himself how he and others had become disenchanted with their adopted country. He felt the pressures of increased racism, increased profiling by local officials, and a sense of not belonging to a society that on the outside begged to be viewed as inclusive and yet was as closed as a dead man's casket. "Malik, I took my 3.5 GPA in chemical engineering and left UCLA after my junior year. Two years later, I met your mother."

Soon thereafter, Abdul and Christina were the happy parents of a new baby boy.

Christina Barnes was not who one expected a man from a traditional Muslim family to marry. But Christina was not a traditional American woman, either. Christina had grown up in Washington State. She had enjoyed a middle class lifestyle in a liberal American family. Christina's parents were quick to teach her that all men and women, no matter their faiths were all part of the fabric of life. Christina's father often told her, "If one string of the fabric is weak and is not supported by the other threads, then the fabric itself is weak and will ultimately rip." Christina allowed this principle to guide her through interactions with others.

Abdul was happy to see his wife already home from work as he and Malik walked up to their two-bedroom apartment. He told his son, "go inside and give Mommy a real big hug." Malik looked back at his father. "I will give her the biggest hug anyone can give", and burst through the front door into his mother's open arms.

At other times, things were rough on the young couple. Christina worked two jobs in order to supplement Abdul's meager earnings from the used-car business. A certified medical assistant at the local free clinic, she also worked the 5 – 11 shift at the local hospital three evenings a week. This did not leave much time for anything else. Christina told her son and husband "I didn't cook tonight because I thought you'd probably filled up on Dodger dogs and soda." Abdul confirmed her suspicion. Malik yelled out, "I had two hotdogs, one soda, and a pack of sour Skittles." Christina let out a loud laugh as she knew the impact of all of the sugar on a child would mean no sleep for the parents. Even through all of the tough times, the couple still managed to provide a warm and loving environment for their only child.

Abdul wanted more children, and Christina knew this. However, they both agreed that as long as they were in their current financial situation, they would not bring more children into the world unless they could provide equally for each.

Christina had seen too many young families visiting the clinic suffering more from the psychosocial ills of not being prepared to care for their multiple children than from some type of physical ailment. The mental stress brought on from the lack of not having the necessary financial resources to care for a family was rampant in the population served by the clinic where Christina worked. She often wondered why people made choices to bring children into a world of suffering when they themselves were suffering from a lack of resources to provide for themselves. But yet they came, and continued to come, from generation to generation. Children had children who themselves were not prepared to provide a nurturing environment and certainly not able to give their own child the head start needed to compete for scarce resources identified as those things needed to be successful by a capitalist society.

Christina knew she and Malik would hold to their belief that one should be able to care for his family without becoming dependent on the governmental system. She also knew that some needed the support of her clinic and the government. To her this was fine as she knew, at some point and time, many could need a helping hand; however, one should not allow this assistance to become a crutch.

Her job at the local hospital consisted mainly of checking patients' vital signs and changing bed pans. It was a job she did not look forward to doing, but it helped pay the bills and provide the things she and her husband determined were needed to sustain the lifestyle they desired for their child, Malik. Malik was her evening star. She knew, she and Abdul would do almost anything to ensure he shone as brightly as any natural star in the sky.

Christina had researched the cost and educational demands of working toward her registered nurse's degree. She and Abdul agreed that this was a logical path for her to take. She loved her husband and respected him dearly as he always attempted to allow her to live out her dreams. She wished the same for Abdul and often became saddened thinking of the reasons that had led to his leaving the local university.

America was a diamond mine for those born with the tools, resources, and the systemic favor granted to those whose skin color gave them "one up" on the rest; however, for those anything other than white middle class, America could be a West Virginia coal mine, harboring death and despair as they mined its depths. It was a known fact that many of the well to do families in the United States had received their wealth through generational hand me downs. Whether their money was made on the backs of the poor slaves in the South or the immigrants from Europe, the white upper class in America for the most part had not earned their spoils, and

yet they continued to choose to adopt laws and policies that

assured the next generation too would benefit from their ancestor's

thievery.

As gas prices continued to rise, combined with local job

losses, the market for used cars was drying up as Americans had

less money to spend even on items that were used. American

companies moved more jobs offshore, so the ability of lower

middle class Americans to make a living wage was reduced.

Abdul didn't fault the companies. He knew from his college

economic classes that they were driven by earning revenue at the

lowest cost. Profits generated earnings, and earnings guaranteed

the top executives their eight-figure salary and compensation

packages. He could not fault anyone for striving to gain as much.

Abdul visited the mosque less frequently as his need for

more income increased. The mosque was a beautifully appointed

building. Its white walls and green dome caused one to relax and

give himself to the great Almighty Allah. On this day many

thoughts were running through Abdul's head; one, being taking on

a second job. He resented the fact that he could not earn enough money to allow his wife to reduce her workload. He loved his wife and child dearly and would work to the death to ensure both remained safe and comfortable at the highest levels of support he could provide. Tonight Abdul would visit the mosque once again to ask his God for assistance, strength, and guidance. That was the least he could ask and the least he would expect for his enduring faith. For many of his fellow countrymen, the faith had been driven to an extreme level since things had changed on that great day in September 2001.

On September 11, 2001, it had been proven that the Great State of Satan could be injured, would bleed, and did have vulnerable spots that if probed could be pierced. From the falling towers in New York City or to the crashed plane at the Pentagon, Americans now knew their protective systems had gaps. Yes, like virus cells, some of his fellow countrymen had found a way to exploit this body politic, America; once the virus had entered, it could become active or lay dormant in the host, dependent on internal conditions there. America's internal condition was constantly changing. But one thing stood steadfast, and that thing was America's support of Israel.

This support caused the greatest friction between America and the Arab world. Plus, America showed no willingness to review the historical reasons for the Middle East's violent past. They were too engrossed in blind support of the Jew. Yes, millions of Jews had been slaughtered throughout history, and yes this was truly unfortunate, but it could not be allowed to rest on the shoulders of the Arab. It was not the Arab who killed the Jew during the Roman Empire's reign, and it truly was not the Arab who killed millions during the Holocaust. But it was the Arab who was the close, easy target for the Jew to use for retribution for history's treatment of him, and it was the Arab who would suffer.

Unknown to many, the Arab had learned, hand changed, had evolved –yes, mutated like a virus to overcome the attempts of the West and of the Jews to wipe its kind from Israel. Certain elements within the Arab culture had mutated and evolved to a point where the West could not identify them as being a threat. This mutation would lay waste to America's greatest pride – its Economy.

This place, America, land of free people was a land where the majority believed their God created humankind as equals. Yet,

America was truly not a place of equality. Conditions were unequal and unjust. True, if you were born with a silver spoon in your mouth, success came with much more ease. But Abdul had grown to understand the real meaning of this statement: the land of the free, the land of the people was, in truth, a land where all rich men were created equal and those less fortunate were no different than the lowly ant in an ant colony, placed in the colony only to serve their master the queen until their use was no longer productive and their value replaced by the next generation.

He frequently wondered, how could the rich not provide for the poor, the disenfranchised, and the people on whom they continued to build their foundation of wealth? What answers to that question Allah would place in his heart tonight, he wondered silently.

As he entered the mosque many of his friends were gathered tonight. He also sensed an upbeat spirit in the air. Many of his friends were smiling and chatting as they waited for the call to evening prayers. Abdul moved towards the right side of the large prayer room to get closer to several of his friends from the neighborhood. Much of the discussion centered on the day's events, information received from relatives in the homeland, and plans each was making for the future. At that moment, the call to prayer began and each man moved to his regular place to pray. Only tonight, the prayer leader would include special chants of which only a few in the room would understand the true meaning.

When Abdul returned home, he found his wife sound asleep. She was his love, his life. He would do anything to protect her. He wanted to talk, but refrained from awakening her. Something did not feel right with him tonight. Instead of his visit and prayers at the Mosque making him feel comfortable and at ease, something in the back of his mind told him all was not right. What could it be?

Chapter 2 – Cause and No Effect

The United States of America is like a body, a living organism. It has a nervous system; Congress and the 50 state legislatures, a cardiovascular system; the country's highways, and also a digestive system; the industrial complex, which converts raw materials into the energy needed to operate its great economic engine. Over the past century, urban sprawl combined with limited state and federal funding had created an expanding energy grid now in disrepair and under-secured. Millions of miles of power lines carried the energy that warmed American homes, providing light so there was never darkness, and created cities that never slept.

The United States of America's power grid is divided into regions, and the larger regions are subdivided into smaller sub-regions. Like a great snake, the power grid cuts through forest, farmland, cities, and country towns. Only recently had the American leadership and corporate elites realized the importance of burying the power grid instead of continuing to hang it high above the ground. Not only would burying the cable prevent damage during the harsh winters in the North and Midwest, it would also prevent damage during the South Atlantic hurricane season and to the military, a buried cable was one less thing for a terrorist to target.

Unfortunately, only a fraction of the power grid is buried. Power substations, backup generators, and other support systems are perched above ground with only chain-link fences for protection. Actually, the fences are there to protect the unwary resident rather than the equipment. In addition, the fences protects the power company against liability should someone decide to scale the fence and touch a power line carrying 50,000 volts of electricity.

America has a long story-filled history concerning its power grid. Many have heard of the summer blackouts in the Northeast and the failed Enron Corporation's generated blackouts in California. However, America's memory is as short as a winter day. Once a story's fifteen seconds of fame passes, something else is fed to the American psyche by the media. Old stories don't sell; the citizens' need constant updates of new material to keep their interest in order for the news corporations to drive their commercial appeal and corporate financial well-being.

After working for Pacific Coast Power for fifteen years, Youssef Aziz was in line to become the executive officer of the power utility company's western division. Youssef was the first in his family to enter college in this new world. Graduating from the University of Southern California with a degree in electrical engineering, he had worked his entire life to this point to repay his mother and father for the risk they had taken in order to escape persecution. His father and mother entered the country after the first great Gulf War. Fearing persecution from Saddam's henchmen for assisting the infidels, at the conclusion of the War, Youssef's father packed up his family and fled to the American Embassy in Iraq, seeking asylum. Asylum being granted, he relocated to California where he felt opportunities and their new community would welcome him and his family. The young Youssef quickly acclimated to the new environment, making friends with his American neighbors.

Youssef entered his office on a day filled with promise. Unfortunately, had the announcement been made much earlier, he would have been a lock for the job. Youssef put up with plenty of negativism from his co-workers during his climb to the top. The day after that fateful morning in September 2001, he thought his life and career had come to an end. How could he be made to feel as though he should have known of the plot, the plot by a few to affect the lives of the many? Yes, the ability of the plotters of the attack on the World Trade Center to enact their plan with chilling effectiveness showed once again that the followers of Allah were superior to the Christian infidels. However, he was not part of the plot and should not bear the burden of the outcome of the plotters' action. Although the burden was great, he was too driven to allow this difference in beliefs to stand in his way of obtaining what his new countrymen called the American Dream: a very big bank account.

"Good morning Ms. Jones how are thing going in the office this morning", Youssef asked his secretary. Ms. Jones responded, "All his well sir and your calendar is pretty deceit today." Jessica Jones was a well-dressed 62-year-old grandmother of ten, who was intent on not letting her age become her defining characteristic. Always well dressed and groomed, she could make any man's father's heartbeat flutter like a butterfly on a midsummer night breeze. Yes, Youssef allowed himself to think, this woman had definitely broken many men along the way. She was his right hand and she viewed Youssef as a son. She admired his work ethic and the way he ensured she was treated well by the company's leadership. She would do anything to assure that he climbed the company's corporate ladder.

Ms. Jones was the mother of five children. Her three sons attended Morehouse University in Atlanta, Georgia. Her twin daughters decided to attend school together at the University of Arizona. She was proud of her children, especially given the fact that their father had died well before the children reached adolescence. Now, she motioned for Youssef to make his move towards the boardroom. She was excited, as she knew he was prepared to take the next step in his career. Yes, it was time.

Once seated at the long board room table, he awaited those expected words from the board chairperson's mouth announcing him as the new chief executive. "Youssef, we are extremely proud of your many accomplishments and excellent leadership shown during your tenure", stated the board chairperson. "Our organization's financial outcomes have grown and you and your strategic leadership are directly responsible for many of our achievements." "However, we will be announcing a different direction as if relates to the new chief executive and therefore, you do not fit in our long term corporate plan. We would love for you to continue in your current role and work with the new leadership to continue our company's prosperous trends," quipped the chairperson. The news hit him like a mortar shell. The nausea he felt was not due to any biological agent. It was caused by the words just uttered by his superior. The job he had worked and dedicated himself to, had just been handed to a junior manager, an infidel, a blue-eyed devil, a man ill prepared to do the job. Youssef knew this was the job he needed in order to achieve those things his father and mother never had the opportunity to gain. However, it would not be his to have. After the news, Youssef left the office to allow his feelings to settle. He always did this when the job generated stress.

A drive through the countryside eased his anger and tension. It also allowed him to develop strategies that solved most of the work problems he had faced during his ascendance to his current position. However, today as he drove the countryside, the thoughts of his recent teachings from his far away Imam went through his mind. As he drove, he observed those things he knew so much about, the power lines, the substations, and the electrical grid. As he drove he thought to himself, "Why would the infidels do this to me?" Instead of becoming calmer, he became angrier. How could the infidels steal his job? How could they place another infidel in his place? Was this the doing of the moron President? Was this the doing of their God? The God who taught the infidels to treat all men as equals and yet, throughout his life in his adopted land, he consistently saw the opposite of these teachings. However, Allah's followers had been taught to expect this, to expect the blue-eyed devil to stop him short of his goal, to stop him because of the fear they had of persons who did not look like them.

A virus can lie dormant in a host's body for years. The virus that causes herpes is capable of causing outbreaks years after the initial infection. Long after the person spreading the disease has affected many more people. Viruses are simple microorganisms. Consisting primarily of strains of ribonucleic acid (RNA), a virus is capable of moving, feeding and possibly a primitive type of thinking. Viruses have been around since the beginning of time. Even today with the numerous drugs, viruses are still seen as an entity to be controlled, not defeated. Viruses are able to mutate, to change their genetic makeup in order to adapt to different environments. The human scientist had designed multiple attack strategies to address the need to protect the masses against the many viruses that had shown the ability to move across different species. The virus is truly something to be respected and destroyed. Human kind had done neither.

Pharmaceutical companies for years had developed drug regimens that led to the dependency of the host's body on their drugs, but the outcome was still the same after the expenditure of thousands and even millions of dollars – Death! As had been speculated by many, but never proven true, drug companies did not wish to develop remedies for death. Yes, abate death but never end the process of death.

The extension of life gave them the opportunity to use their drugs to treat, not cure. The extension of life resulted in the utilization of their drugs. The use of their drugs by the masses led to significant stock growth and the acquisition of many dead American presidents in the form of American currency to fill the corporate elite's pocketbooks and bank accounts. The failure of the system was a failure en-masse. The failure to develop ways to eradicate viruses was also a failure to develop methods that could be adapted from the microscopic world to the macro world, the world of Youssef Aziz. A terrorist operates like a virus. There was so much to be learned from the microscopic world, but as usual the leadership of the free world was focused more on making money. Ironically, so was Youssef as he had learned well his new culture, and his complicity increased his anger at not getting his rightful promotion. It was complicated.

Youssef had lain dormant and thus was not under the microscope of the United States' intelligence establishment. He had learned to act, smell, and even talk like an American. Seen in public, he was just another well-tanned American male heading towards late-age skin cancer. But Youssef's skin color was not due to a desire to be American. It was his genetics. He was Arab and proud of his heritage. He used his intelligence and knowledge of the American system to help his fellow countrymen from afar.

Oh, how misinformed and unaware he found his host. Americans were quick to forget, quickly to love, and quick to want to earn a fast dollar. This desire to earn money and acquire materialistic things led to a lowering of one's defenses. Americans would connect with anyone who could earn them more money, even if it was illegal, so long as the illegality of the event could be masked from the authorities. Thus, those wishing like the virus in a human's body could easily be protected by the United States' systems that were meant to protect it from harm.

For years, Youssef and his family had blended into the American fabric. Taking care of his aging parents, wife, and kids, he appeared to be an immigrant who had achieved the American Dream. He regularly wondered why others had not been able to achieve as he had. He wondered why the African American, who had been given all types of breaks, laws to protect him, and social welfare as an economic foundation had not broken the chains of slave bondage. He always came to the same conclusion. If they or any other ethnic group did not want to take advantage of the bounty laid out by this great country, he surely would and would share it with people who could exact pain on those who had caused pain for his Arab countrymen.

Unlike the body's immune system, the United States' intelligence system was slow to react to outside pathogens. Again this was due to the desire of the United States intelligence system to bring in more money for the elite. These pathogens; persons intent on causing harm to the American way of life were allowed in through numerous openings. Whether through air, sea, or land, immigrants with good and bad intentions flowed in by the millions. Unfortunately, Youssef Aziz was not identified as a pathogen until it was too late -- much too late.

Sometimes the environmental condition of a host's body causes triggers that activate a dormant virus. Whether the trigger is stress, chemical imbalances, or other environmental changes within the host, the virus is triggered to awake. Each time the virus goes from dormant to active phase; the host's body is compromised and further weakened. At some point, the body is unable to mount a sufficient response to the virus and is consumed. The awakening of the virus causes fear in the body, just as the announced return of cancer generates fear in the cancer survivor's mind. So too is the fear of the American as he awaits the return of the terrorist, America's cyclical cancer.

After being passed up for the CEO position for Pacific Power, Youssef knew what must be done. He sensed the tide changing. He would act. He knew the land of Satan was vulnerable. Thousands of miles of unprotected power lines and transmission stations were easy targets. He had the maps and the knowledge -- and now the motivation. A truckload of aluminum foil would be enough to short-circuit any remote transmission station. A few well-placed bombs could darken the entire western half of the country. Before acting and sharing the information with his contact, Youssef would notify his boss of a long-planned vacation to Jordan. Only Youssef would know that Jordan was not his final destination.

Yes, old "Blue Eyes" stole his dream job and cheated him of the satisfaction of seeing the happiness in his parent's eyes, but he had amassed sufficient numbers of dead presidents; U.S. dollars, to allow his family to live comfortably in his homeland. The information needed by his contact would arrive well after he and his family had settled into his new home. He would figure out later how to contact Ms. Jones. She had covered his back for years, and now he had to desert her. But sometimes the importance of action exceeds the desire for emotional connections. He would act; he hoped the good people like Ms. Jones would not feel the heat of the fires that would soon burn.

Youssef knew it was time to engage his cloak. His name and the names of his family members would be changed, and they would transit through several countries before settling into their final home. During each transit, passports and names would be changed in order to reduce the chances that Interpol and the FBI would find them.

Chapter 3 – Floodgates

Unknown too many Americans, the news media is a paid surrogate of the United States' government. Since its early years in the eighteenth century, the news media has received billions of dollars to provide propaganda to support the position of the United States government. In today's terminology, that's "Spin Control."

The spin on any topic is key to the government's ability to control the masses. The forefathers knew that information would be one factor in allowing the elites to subdue and direct the desires of the minority. Becoming more like a colony of ants, people followed the chemical trail of their leadership without giving a second thought to the direction of the country. Yes, some attempted to provide a dissenting opinion. But those ants were quickly attacked by the masses or their voices were not strong enough to be heard by those near the queen ant.

A President who wanted only good news now led America. Although his handlers knew his spending policies were moving the country in a direction that would imperial the future, his administration's goal was to achieve short-term outcomes of benefit to those who had supported his climb to the highest office.

One of the administration's greatest strengths was its ability to spin today's issues. His adept use of "spin control" allowed the administration to lay down an alluring chemical trail so the masses would follow his policies and eliminate the chance that anyone in the Administration to question their validity. This philosophy of spin control not just practiced by the current President, but by previous administrations had done enough damage to America's credibility that now caused Youssef to set his retributive plan in motion.

Like the skin, the borders of America were open. This had been known for many decades. Thousands of illegal immigrants moved across the America's borders with Canada and Mexico, bringing with them a desire to achieve greater financial wealth than they could in their pinched, stratified economies in their home country. This movement benefited the U.S. and Mexico greater than it benefited Canada because Canada had a reputable financial standing and an ability to create jobs for its people.

Mexico was a different story. Like every country, it had its elite. The persons in control of Mexico's government; the queen ants, were not the native Indians who had lived in this area of the hemisphere for thousands of years. Like America, Mexico had been invaded by outside forces from thousands of miles away. The Spanish Conquistadors who had followed Christopher Columbus to the new world had settled into this Central Region of the Americas, bringing with them their religious beliefs, weaponry, and diseases. Soon the native Indians in this region were vanquished by all three.

Today, those descendants of the invading Spanish armies lead Mexico. Those descendants rule Mexico without regard to the needs of the poor native Indian. Unlike the invading Europeans to the north in the United States, Mexico did not choose to put the Indians on reservations only to watch them die. The Spanish interlopers allowed the Indians to live among them without providing the necessary systems to allow them to improve their stake in life. In Mexico, the vast majority of the poor is made up of native Indians. In many Mexican towns and cities, one can easily discriminate between Spanish descendants and Native Indian descendants.

In response to this economic imbalance, many Mexican residents (Native Indian) chose to create their own "Middle

Passage," as thousands died crossing the border into America. Like the body's integumentary system, the deserts of America's Southwest proved to be an excellent protector of the country's internal systems, just as the human body has the ability to repel attacks from invading microorganisms. With any attack on the body, when microorganism attack through cuts in the skin, mucous systems, or other pathways, the human body brings on a counter-attack by producing millions of antibodies and white blood cells to attack the invading microbes. If the body is in good health, many times it is able to win the battle.

However, if the body is weak or the microbe too strong, the body's defenses can be overwhelmed. This is true as well for America's ability to control its borders. Like the body's skin, the borders and the deserts can be overrun if the invading army of microbes is either too numerous or has mutated to repel the attack from America's systems of protection. Whether the counter attack comes from the deserts or the northern border with Canada, too many microbes invading would insure some would get through to begin establishing healthy cells. The concern of many Americans was which of these cells would create cancers in the form of terrorist sleeper cells intent on destroying America from within.

An attack from Mexican immigrants is not a major concern of the American government. America's supposedly brain, Congress, was too self-involved with making money for their constituencies and preserving their jobs. The constituencies had become powerful systems in the lives of the Congress. It was these groups who control the legislation debate in Washington. The inability of the border patrol and other government agencies to stem the influx of illegal aliens is directly related to the billions of dollars companies made on the backs of poor immigrants, the Native Indians from Mexico and South America who's only quest was to make their lives and the lives of their family members in their home country better. A direct correlation also existed in the financial strength of the Mexican economy as billions of dollars flowed back across the border. The Mexican government's biggest export, cheap Indian labor pays great dividends as it yields billions of dollars in U.S. currency for the Mexican economy. With an exchange rate of ten pesos to every U.S. dollar, the gain for the Mexicans and their bankers and other elites who derived their heritage from Spain was very evident. As it was with the American Indian and now with the South American Indian, someone from the outside in this case; Spain, was now using its control to maximize financial benefit.

The open border with Mexico and Canada has indeed ceded its ability to identify harmful pathogens that use this river of cheap labor as a pathway into America. Through this cut, the pathogens; immigrants from faraway eastern countries, could carry out attacks against the United States. Many more have passed through and now are poised to further the cause of Islam. Yes, America has been cut, a self-inflicted wound driven wider and deeper by its desire to generate more money for the rich on the backs on the poor, namely the Native Indian from Mexico.

However, this time, the obsessive drive for dead presidents will cause many Americans to question whether death, not life, is the better option. Fear, not death, is the ultimate weapon. Living with fear causes stress on the human body, which eventually results in a breakdown of the body's protective systems. As the stress continues, the body's defenses weaken; giving pathogens the ability to override the body's defenses. The pathogens that have entered American's cut will attempt to override these final

defenses and will in time initiate activities to begin a major assault

on America.

Chapter 4: Hear No Evil, Speak No Evil, and See No Evil

Abdul arose early for work. It was the end of the month and he wanted to be certain that he stood a chance of selling at least two cars. This would push him past his monthly quota and would assure him of his incentive bonus. He had plans for this money. His wife and child had gone without for so long. However, with Allah's blessing, he would reach and surpass his goal and receive the payout so he could bring happiness into his family's life.   The drive to work was uneventful.

Abdul parked his car in the employee parking lot and quickly entered the car showroom. His sales manager and two of his co-workers were already there discussing the day's news. The war in his homeland had gone on for years. The Syrians had attempted to resolve the fragmented peace in Lebanon by stationing their troops on the border with Israel. This strategy had maintained the peace for twenty-five years.

Unfortunately, peace in the Middle East is not a static state. History records that this region of the world has been at war for four thousand years. From Abraham to Isaac, from Moses to

Joshua, this region has been at war. Tribes with common bloodlines have fought and killed each for generations.

The Jews' relationship with America had always kept America only a trigger finger's reaction from being involved, but America's experience in Vietnam made the American public wary of getting involved in Middle Eastern conflicts. From its last experience east of the Bosporus, America had learned that it is easier to enter the house than it is to leave. The last conflict cost the country, especially the unfortunate families eight thousand dead American soldiers and a significant portion of its prestige and standing in the world, which had taken years to repair. The Syrians and Israelis had been at war again for five years. The war was not a full out attack by either country, it consisted primarily of border skirmishes between small patrols.

Both countries knew a full-blown war would explode into an enormous regional firestorm. With its return as a superpower, Russia moved quickly to buy favor with its former Middle Eastern allies by restocking their stores of arms. This had come at the displeasure of the Americans and Israelis. But since Russia had vast oil supplies, both America and Israel had to step carefully when dealing with the Russians. No longer could they depend on the Saudis to increase their output of oil, since the Saudis had known for several years their supply of oil was drying up. Yes, things in the world had changed.

Abdul greeted his co-workers with an excited; "hello" as he entered the showroom His entire sales team was excited. Abdul sales manager told the team, "Car sales were rebounding in their region. He said, "I feel today would be no different from the past several days where we exceeded our sales forecast". All had maintained good sales rates and were expecting to make their monthly quota. Abdul had settled into his cubicle when the phone rang. It was Mashir. Abdul thought it strange that Mashir would call him at this time of the day or even at all.

He and Mashir had been friends, actually just acquaintances, since high school. Both had gone their separate ways, but Abdul had always supported those he felt were in need of help. He never would turn his back on his fellow man, whether he was an infidel or a true believer. In Abdul's mind, all of his God's people deserve the best and the love of their fellow man.

Mashir was upbeat. He told Abdul, "my brother, great things are happening and I wish you would join me in my quest to show the infidels the wonders of Islam." Mashir continued, stating, "Allah is the only God, the great God and the infidels were wrong to believe in a God that allowed people to suffer." Mashir asked Abdul, "Brother please join me after work so we can talk about these things." Abdul, knowing this would be a long day, told his old friend, "Mashir, I will call you later and we will spend time together if my day goes well." Mashir gave him his cell phone number 888-4630, and Abdul wrote it down.

Chapter 5 – Rain

Another rainy Saturday with nothing to do—well, almost nothing to do. Zachary Carson Wilson was about to leave his house to head to the base when the phone rang. His unit commander was on the line and told Zachary, "Drills had been canceled". The Unit Command told Zachary, "It seemed the folks back in Washington needed to have a conference call to discuss the latest information feed on the threats Zachary's unit tracked for the past twelve months". Yes, these were new times. America had been invaded, but not with tanks, warships or airplanes. His country had invited the enemy in. The country's borders had been opened by the government asking all to come to the land of the free, home of the brave, home of apple pie and the American Dream. Americans - well, the Pilgrim descendants were a gullible bunch, he thought.

Having successfully brought Africans to this country hundreds of years ago and assimilated them into the American fabric, once again the thought process was to allow other immigrant groups in. They too would acclimate to the culture of their new home and would grow to love this country as their own.

Though thousands of Africans were brought here unwillingly

through the "Door of No Return" on

Goree Island in Senegal, Africa, and definitely with no way to

return to their beloved homeland, these new visitors to America

had both the financial means to return to their homelands and did

not feel compelled to join the American fabric of life. Their goal

for coming to America was simple - to put as many American

dollars in their pockets as they could possibly carry.

For the past several months, Zachary's task force,

commonly referred to as Task Force Seek had been hot on the trail

of an extremist group called "Scarlet Badge," SB for short. It

seemed Scarlet Badge had been identified as one of the groups in this country with the finances and intellectual know-how to cause disruption of the great American engine – The Economy.

Zachary's unit commander told him, "The amount of chatter had increased steadily since the election." It was hard for Zachary to understand how his country could once again re-elect a moron to the highest office of the free world. Arrogance had its place, but not in this country's Oval Office. One thing America did not need was a President who made enemies just by his insane, confused words and aggressive actions. Too many times this President had stuffed his moral value system down the throats of other countries and their people. At some point, Zachary knew this impulsive behavior would play havoc with the stability of his country and the safety of its people.

As Zachary checked the status of the secure line, he poured himself another cup of coffee. He had become addicted to the quick jolt of energy derived from one of the world's most available legalized drugs, caffeine. America had its rules and its rights. Behind the nicotine in cigarettes, alcohol in our mixed drinks and the caffeine in our coffee, our leaders chose the drugs that would be allowed to generate money for the capitalist elite. He heard his unit commander's voice and settled into his favorite chair. He knew instinctively this would not be a short call.

Zachary Wilson had meandered through life for the better part of his adolescence and young adulthood. He was the youngest of three brothers and had benefited from the fact that by the time he became a teenager, his parents were tired or very trusting that he had watched the ups and downs of his two older brothers and knew how to make good decisions.

He worked hard to hide the fact that he was an intelligent individual. Having scored high on IQ tests and his SAT, he felt it was too much of a burden of responsibility to be identified as intelligent. But as he grew older and became more involved in extracurricular activities, his leadership and intelligence could not be hidden. Still, had it not been for an overbearing history teacher, Zachary probably would not have attended college. His first two years at the University were nothing to write home about. To this day, Zachary didn't understand why his father and mother didn't slam him when his poor grades came home.

The A's and B's that came so easily in high school melted away to B's and C's. A major part of the problem was that

Zachary did not see the importance of retaking subjects he felt had no bearing on his future livelihood, whatever that may have been. He constantly asked his friends, why it was a requirement to take English, Algebra, and other courses that were similar to the courses he had taken in high school. Given his attitude, it is easy to see why C's and D's became the norm. Things changed for Zachary once he was able to declare a major and take courses he was interested in. Having scored his highest grades in the sciences, he was quick to declare a major in biology, hoping one day to become a cardiologist. Zachary was amazed how one organ could hold the balance of life while operating on one-half volt of electricity.

His unit commander, Colonel John McIntosh told Zachary, "One of the Scarlet Badge's main assets left the country on vacation." Zachary noted this on his Ipad. He would follow up on this information later in the week. The contact Youssef Aziz had been watched for some time. Although Youssef Aziz gave the appearance of being an immigrant who had come to America, climbed the ladder of success, and was contributing to the Economy's success, Zachary and his group knew otherwise. From early in his young adulthood, "Youssef Aziz had maintained contacts with terrible people who wanted America to suffer, American blood spilled in the streets and he knew the right people who had the financial resources to make their visions a reality", Zachary told his commander.

For years Youssef Aziz had sympathized with groups associated with Al Qaeda. Zachary told Commander McIntosh that, "his group's forensic accountants had determined Youssef had channeled millions of dollars to groups throughout the Middle East over the past ten years." Zachary further stated, "What was concerning was the fact that the latest deciphered information indicated one of the potential targets for the next attack might be America's infrastructure – utilities, water, food, health care or public facilities." Even more disturbing, Zachary continued "Was the facts that were pointing towards involvement of key personnel in industries that could affect key infrastructure systems."

The problem with information is that it can overwhelm any computer system and definitely any human. Zachary knew to connect the dots; to connect the lines took too much time. In addition, America's legal system due process protects everyone. If this were Mexico, Columbia, Russia, or China, just the whisper of being involved in treachery was enough for the authorities to bring someone in for intense questioning. Zachary knew that in these countries, the intensity of the questioning was dependent on how quickly the person gave the authorities the information they needed and no suspect could request a lawyer. A lawyer was not allowed to be their "mouthpiece." Their own mouth had to save them. If they did not provide the information, they could disappear along with their family.

In America, the person "of interest" would be back home for Monday night football before his buddies opened the first can of Bud Lite. Zachary Carson Wilson thought, Don King had it right, "Only in America, Only in America."

Even so, Zachary knew he would need to push his group harder. To connect the dots and cover all bases fast and competently they had to achieve a successful interdiction of the terrorists' next plan before it could be launched. Colonel McIntosh concluded their call with his usual "Be careful" speech. Zachary, as always told his command and old friend, "We will be careful, as careful as the situation allowed." Colonel McIntosh served many years with the man on the other end of the phone line and he knew, once the warrior within was released, anyone or anything seen as an enemy would see the light of day – their life, come to an end. Zachary pondered after he hung up the phone, "The only problem with trying to determine the next target or what the enemy was thinking was that America offered so many targets. A car driven at seventy miles an hour on a busy interstate highway could be a terrorist's weapon, if handled in the correct way." Unfortunately, he instinctively knew his team would need luck or major assistance if they were to make a break before the next attack occurred.

After the call, Zachary called his wife, Karla, to let her know he was going away. Karla responded with her usual, "You have always got to be the one to save humanity, why don't you save your damn family? You expect me to forgive, to forget, and I don't care what the Bible says, I cannot turn off the pain of your failure to protect my family. I don't care what you saw growing up, this is not your childhood family and I'm not your damn mother!" Zachary felt the tingle run down his neck as he knew the next several minutes would be full of Karla's blasting him for his chosen career. She continued, "And if you spent as much time engaged in my needs and your kids' needs, then our family would be successful. Your ass is always running around here trying to save someone else. Do you know your kids, hell I don't care if you know me! I don't love you and I hate the damn day I met your ass. Yeah, you fooled me and I hate I married you!" she concluded. Karla blasting him was constant for things they did and yet, the kids were successful, involved in multiple activities and they constantly received remarks from those who met their children that they were behaved and respectful. It did not help the situation that the kids were on their school's honor roll. Zachary wondered, "Why have I stayed in this situation, why can't I walk away, why can't I walk away?"

Zachary told Karla, "I am going away soon. I don't know when I will be back, but you know who to contact should emergencies arise. I truly hate you feel the way you do about me. I cannot redo the errors I have made in the past. The only thing I can do for you and the kids now is to make your present and your future better than yesterday." Karla knew this was going to be another long deployment and in her mind she really didn't care. She told Zachary, "All I ever wanted was a supporting spouse, who would support my aspirations. I didn't sign up to be Betty Crocker to General George Custer." For a fleeting moment, Zachary laughed silently to himself as he wondered if he would follow the same faith as General Custer and would Karla be his Crazy Horse, one of the Indian leaders. Her goals and Zachary's career constantly met in conflict, centering more on which person in the family would excel while the other watched. Karla quipped, "No longer did women want to be cared for, they wanted to care for themselves." She said, "Women today are not afraid to tell you guys where to stick it. We don't need you like our mothers needed men back in the olden days, when mom stayed home and the man was free to roam." Karla knew Zachary didn't feel this way, but it was something internal to her that caused her to be jealous of her husband's seemingly easy upbringing. She constantly compared her childhood to his and consistently found ways to attack his family's environment as the reason he is the man he is. She wanted more in life than watching someone else succeed; this included her husband, and felt her early childhood had not afforded her the same opportunities others experienced. As an adult with the means to attain her desires, she would stop short of nothing to achieve them.

This pressure on their marriage meant they were constantly at each other regarding the smallest matters. A bill not being paid, five minutes late for picking up a child from practice, or the slightest misstep led to a tirade that would push Zachary to the brink of his sanity. Karla was intelligent, vibrant and fun to be around sometimes, now the sometimes had become fewer recently. It was a testament to Zachary's ability to focus that he was able to keep control not only of his need to be a good father, but also to excel at what he did best, hunting bad guys. However, Zachary too regretted his outburst, anger and threats that typically happen when things were stressful on the job. He had to fight for world peace and carry the baggage of many and could not come home to a place of peace and solitude due to bad things he had done earlier in his marriage.

Karla asked, "Why of all of the people in the United States military did he always have to be the one chasing after the bad guys?" She knew the answer to this question, but ended up asking it over and over again. She told her husband, "I have dreams and desires that as long as we are together and you continue to allow the military to be your family will go unfulfilled." This attitude or lack of support from, as Zachary took it only added to the depth of his despair. How could he; the one who could make split-second decisions, impact persons' lives without their knowledge, be so powerless against this foe, his wife? But something was wrong with this mindset; why was she a foe? Marriage was supposed to be a partnership. Quitting his marriage was not an option, as he did not know the word. As a youth, he had allowed his desire for instant gratification to quit sports teams, jobs and other initiatives. Hind sight had shown him these decisions were wrong, short sighted and cost him severely in the long run. So, he was destined to remain in a painful situation uncommon to him and frustrating, and yet he remained calm. To the outside world all seemed normal.

But things were not normal in the Wilson household and Zachary did not know how much more he could take. His wife had changed, and he wondered if her unwillingness to forgive his past infidelity was embedded in some childhood event that caused forgiveness to be a word foreign to Karla. Could his wife's upbringing, devoid of love and happiness have caused her to be afraid of accepting happiness and even of having the desire to be truly close to someone? Could Karla not come close enough to him to accept his personal failures and regain her trust? Zachary's life was full of trials and remorse, and he knew he needed the support of the one he had chosen to be with him for the remainder of his life to help him through the darkness of temptations.

However, when the one you have who is chosen to hold your hand fails to be able to provide the support needed, then in the darkness the potential was there to always grab the wrong hand. Zachary knew he had grabbed the wrong hands in the past, but yet he also knew he had reached a point in his life where he would fight the temptation of the dark in order to produce a positive future for his three children and hopefully, Karla.

Chapter 6: Convergence Zones

Convergence zones are formed when two opposing forces come together. At the point of contact, pressures build until one force overwhelms the other. During normal convergence in the case of tectonic oceanic plates, typically one plate will slide underneath the other, releasing pressure and adverting disaster. In cases where neither plate chooses to give, immense pressures increase until both plates surge upwards. When this happens, great amounts of ocean water can be displaced, resulting in massive ocean waves called tsunamis.

Convergence zones are also formed in the ocean when two strong ocean currents meet. Ocean convergence zones are marked by temperature and water mass characteristics. At these points, like a wind current, warm water rises as cold water sinks. These areas are normally major feeding grounds for marine animals since nutrients are brought close to the surface on the up swells of warm water. Submariners have long known that these zones also are great at masking ocean sounds and thus are great hiding places to await the right time to attack an unsuspecting surface ship or another submarine, or to unleash a nuclear arsenal on an unsuspecting country.

Zachary heard Karla upstairs telling the kids it was time to get up and prepare for school. He smiled, knowing this was going to be a difficult job for his wife. None of his kids were morning people. His baby daughter, seven years old told, her mother, "It's only 7 o'clock in the morning, please wake me up at 7:10." Zachary thought, even seven year olds know how to press the parental snooze button winning ten minutes in an early morning convergence zone.

Like the submariners, Zachary knew the terrorists in America had found a convergence zone. To the terrorists, America had made it easy for them to live amongst the populace in plain sight. Unless his team developed a way to read the terrorists sounds within society's diurnal sounds, they did not stand a chance of finding out when and where they would strike next. Convergence zones -- he wished he could find one for himself in order to hide from the problems he faced. For he knew the quiet was only a temporary condition until the enemy his opposing force, decided if it was time for another up swell. Just like a major tsunami, a terrorist up swell in America could kill thousands.

Karla asked Zachary, "Are you ok if I move some of our money from the interest bearing account into the credit union where it would accrue more interest?" Karla didn't know that Zachary truly adored his wife and her business savvy. He had attempted to show his admiration multiple times, but the anger and the negativism had caused him now not to care if she responded positively to his comments and like her, he had shut down. Zachary said, "Sure, Honey that would be fine." Karla was definitely the Chief Executive Officer and Chief Financial Officer of the Wilson family.

Zachary finished packing his bags into his car. Tonight he would fly to Washington to be briefed before meeting his team in Quantico, Virginia. The flight would take four hours, and he thought this would be the last time he would be able to get some rest. From this point forward, he would be in action mode. For Zachary, being in action mode meant the enemy would suffer losses. If the enemy was the virus, then his team was the anti-viral drug that did not need the Federal Drug Administration's approval to act.

The plane landed in Washington at two p.m. EST. A junior lieutenant met Zachary and gave him his briefing papers after the normal salute but did not offer any words of welcome. The lieutenant had received his briefing and knew not to interfere with Zachary Carson Wilson's thought processes when he was in action mode. The young airman could feel the intensity of the soldier he was tasked to transport to the Pentagon. Yes, this man sitting next to him had probably killed and killed silently and quickly. No, this would not be a guy to upset or a guy to antagonize.

As Zachary set in the passenger seat of the government vehicle for the forty-five minute ride to Andrews Air Force base, he knew the traffic would be heavy on I-495, since it was Friday. As he rode, he thought how strange the planners of Washington, DC, and the surrounding metropolitan area never figured out how to design the inner and outer loops around the nation's capitol to improve the flow of traffic. If a major attack ever occurred in DC, the highways would cause the death of many because people would either be killed in the attack or decide to kill each other due to the frustration caused by the gridlock of I-95, I-395, I-295 and I-495 all converging at Springfield, VA.

The meeting between the military and representatives from the White House was scheduled for four p.m. Zachary and Colonel Macintosh briefed the senior Pentagon leadership on what they knew about the current threat from Scarlet Badge. Zachary worked the room like the true leader he was. Everyone knew that Zachary Wilson was going places if he was able to avoid the pitfalls of life. Zachary told the group, "The amount of chatter from Scarlet Badge was increasing, but it was difficult to truly assess what the information meant.

The lack of Arab interpreters and the constant drain on support due to resources being shifted to the President's ever-changing priorities, which in code meant paying off his interest groups, left his group blinded to many of Scarlet Badge's core activities." Zachary didn't allow his frustration to show with the current leadership, but he did throw in the barb by stating, "If the President had listened to us several years ago when we requested the resources to send a interdiction force into Syria, we could have killed some of the bastards who we believe to be behind the things we think are being planned." Zachary's eyes were like laser beams and for several of the White House staffers, his glaze towards them felt as if they had been shot. Zachary's face told the story that his mind thought, but his professionalism didn't allow his mouth to say. Those who he felt were assholes knew that was what his facial expressions were telling them. Zachary's final assessment thought was that something was going to happen. He felt it would happen on American soil, but he was unable to pinpoint a time or place.

Jack Rogers, one of the White House suits, blurted out, "This assessment is a waste of time! You called all of us here to tell us what you could have told us on the phone. It was a tough re-election year, the economy is in the tank and we all could be doing something else rather than listening to a report that tells us nothing!" Jack Rogers was one of those who owed his success his ability to be a leech to anyone or anything that could put money in his pocket. From being the water boy for the high school basketball team to being a supposed friend of a famous basketball player, this guy made a life of telling people what they wanted to hear, not what they needed to hear. One of the major downfalls of the current administration was that the President was surrounded by a protective barrier of wannabe leeches.

Jack Rogers went to Georgetown University, fell in love with the city, and vowed never to leave. He had been able to maintain this vow for the past fifteen years, along the way latching onto the coattails of people who were going places. Zachary leaned over to one of his team members and whispered in this ear, 'This guy is an asshole, worse yet, like used toilet paper." Zachary's teammate almost fell out of his chair but held in his desire to laugh out loud. Delivering zingers was Jack's greatest trait.

To tell the group, Jack added, "I could learn everything reported today by picking up the Washington Post." His tirade went on until one of the more senior White House officials intervened, but the intervention was soft and all of the military people in the room knew the message that was being sent, the same message at the core of the White House's philosophy of engaging the military since the current administration took office. Jack Rogers asked Zachary, "Do you have any additional information more useful than what we have spent the last sixty minutes listening to and if not why not?" The White House was afraid of anyone who posed a threat to its position. Zachary was seen by Rogers to be a threat.

Rogers knew the career military officer would not play the establishment's game which was to find out the truth, then create a solution with the only aim of putting more money into the pockets of the friends of the those inhabiting the White House. Wars had been started for profits before, and the war being fought now was no less than that. Rogers knew if Zachary found out the truth, profiteering by those in power would be exposed. If links were made to the President, threats to the country would become very real. Therefore, the administration exerted every opportunity to control, especially the military.

Information from secret polling showed the President and his policies were not well respected by the military's leadership. These members gave the administration much concern. Jack hurled his final insult: "This short briefing for the White House and could have been handled via a conference call as I have previously stated. The next time you guys want to convene a group such as this, please have more tangible information to present or else don't invite me."

The keen ears of Zachary Wilson, duly noted Rogers' ill-concealed contempt for his team and its work. Zachary knew if chance afforded him the opportunity to meet this Jack "Ass" Rogers guy in person, this civilian for a number of reasons would remember who he was. Zachary knew his group worked hard, but the fact that the current batch of civilians in the White House did not believe in listening only made his team's job more difficult.

After leaving the briefing room, Zachary and Colonel Macintosh left to go downstairs to the Pentagon's Command Operating Center (COC). Colonel McIntosh asked his young warrior, "Are you ok Zachary? Don't let the White House asshole worry you and distract you from your primary goal. We have dealt with these types of individuals throughout our careers and we will not lose this battle to this jerk – Rogers", the Colonel concluded. As they entered the stairwell, he told Zachary, "It is important for those in the forest to sometimes leave the forest to fully appreciate its beauty." Zachary knew what his old friend was trying to say, but felt the Colonel never had full command of his words.

The COC was where data coming in from multiple points of interest was combined into assessment and threat reports. Zachary wanted to talk to the team of interpreters to see if they had been able to analyze and determine what the latest information meant. Things had changed since September 11, 2001, and those whose job it was to protect the masses knew things never could return to the complacency before that memorable day. America's military had grown to trust no one. Recently the military took its share of bumps and bruises as young soldiers had been sent by inept civilian leadership to die early deaths without gain for America. Lies and deceit had become the order of the day as more and more people had been selected to Congress without any knowledge and historical perspective how their decisions would impact America's standing in the world. Too many in Congress today believed a War was something fought by men and women who did not have the financial or intellectual means to go to college out of high school. This lack of understanding and respect had now led the country to brink of utter revolution. Given this fact, the military had taken many things into its own hands without the knowledge of the civilian leadership. One of those things was the secret Project Closed Door. One thing about people, Zachary thought as he entered the stairwell, is that money can buy you just about anything in this new world order.

No longer was it as important to be a true patriot to one's country. Zachary told Colonel McIntosh, "Instead, the philosophy of the global economy is that the entire world is a country, and individual republics are only states of this larger system." So Project Closed Door was really an open door. As China, Russia, and others joined the world economy, their desire for Western-style informatics (computer systems and software) resulted in their buying more and more electronics from companies with different names that were in truth same company.

Zachary told Colonel McIntosh, "The use of different names and the hiding of this fact of their association to a single parent company was done in order to minimize the concern of foreign governments that America controlled the company's direction." The fact that foreign countries such as Russia and China, sworn enemies of the US could now purchase high level technology from American firms his team and the military were sworned to protect bothered him. Zachary stated, "Russia, China,

Great Britain, and a host of other countries had purchased the software used to form the basis of their spy and threat assessment systems from the same American company." His team had developed Project Closed Door after a chance encounter between a U.S. government official with the owner of the company that produced the software. The owner of the company, after many months of courting by the government and the assurance by the Congress of the United States of America that his family would never run the risk of being poor, gave up the information needed to allow American intelligence assets the ability to access the system no matter where it was located.

The software was intelligent and once installed on a host system was programmed to do what ET from the 1980's movie did, phone home. Foreign countries had the intelligence required to block access to their systems from outside sources, but they felt using the new software offered a smaller threat. However, the new software itself was a spy, sending an encrypted message back to the folks at Langley, who then were able to set up the parameters that allowed them to invoke Project Closed Door. America now had the ability to access at any time the spy networks of several foreign governments. Colonel McIntosh told his young warrior, "We have become a paranoid group, and with the paranoia came a shifting of the rules of engagement. I only hope the military does not see the ineptness of the civilian leadership as reason to take further steps to maintain the country's security." This thought sent a cool chill down Zachary's spine as he knew many within the multiple branches of the military too had this concern.

As Zachary got off the elevator, he told Colonel Macintosh, "Go ahead, I need to stop by the "little boys' room" to download the gallon of coffee he drank before the meeting." As he entered the bathroom, he saw Mr. Jack Rogers, the young White House aide who had torn down his group this morning during the briefing. Jack noticed Zachary, but his arrogance kept him from fathoming the threat this presented to him. Jack nodded to Zachary and asked, "Why would someone want to spend the better part of his or her life in the military when so much could be gained in civilian life?" "I really do appreciate your effort to uncover the threats to America, but I just feel the money we are spending on activities such as your program; we saw this morning are not yielding any tangible results, is just not smart. The use of the country's resources on men who still want to play with their toy soldiers is a waste of time, money and other resources."

Zachary's experience had shown him to be respectful of all. He let Jack continue with his assessment of the current situation while Zachary went to the sink to wash his hands before proceeding to the COC. But, Jack made the mistake of putting his hands on Zachary's shoulders to make sure Zachary was listening to what he was saying. The blow to Jack's chest was quick and powerful. Before he knew what happened, Jack found himself on the floor of the bathroom with Zachary extending a hand to help him up. At this point, Jack could see that the angel of death had entered the bathroom and was standing above him with a hand extended. Jack did not know whether to accept the assistance or pick himself up off the floor himself.

He chose to accept the hand, and Zachary lifted his accuser off the floor. "Now Sir, it's your time to listen", Zachary said. But Jack's arrogance returned shortly after his lungs had refilled with oxygen. Before Zachary could explain the threat situations facing the country and what his team was facing, Jack cursed and told Zachary he would be busted down to private first class after he was finished with him. Zachary Wilson knew he needed to set the playing field for this youngster.

Zachary grabbed Jack's throat. "You need to listen very carefully. You can cause problems, but the fact that I am very important to the current team charged with uncovering any plots against America, the fact that the threats to America are real, and the fact that current threat assessments indicate an immediate threat to America means several months or years would pass before disciplinary action was taken against me. By then, the current administration, along with you, Mr. Rogers, will be a bad footnote to the history of America." Zachary went on to tell Rogers, "I have friends who lived in the dark and thrive for the hunt. Now, Mr. Rogers, you can choose, and here are the choices. You threaten me, you threaten my family. Once you enter my family into the equation, you have entered your family into the equation. You choose, sir, but I will do anything in my power to protect my family's well-being. This game between you and me can end now, or you can choose to push the start button and seek disciplinary action against me. As you are making your decision, ask people in the know about who I am. I think if you are capable of making a true assessment of the situation, you will determine

that this situation is best left here in this bathroom with the rest of

the shit that has occurred here today." Seeing the fear in the young

man's face, Zachary knew his point had been made, so he let him

go.

Jack's oxygen supply to his brain had been limited for

about two minutes as Zachary explained the situation, causing him

to slump to the floor again. Zachary washed his hands again and

left the bathroom.

Chapter 7 - Placement

Cold, wind driven snow pelted Washington, DC. The district police officer had driven this patrol route many times in his five-years on the police force. He could tell you the schedules of every homeless person and every lady of the evening within his seven--block patrol area.

There was the White House again on his left though it didn't seem like the place he had viewed in the history books when he was a young boy. Yes, it was white, but it was too massive to be called a house, although it was the home away from home of the leader of the most powerful nation and only remaining superpower of the world. Jones thought how funny it was how a super power could be brought to its knees by countries much smaller, much weaker than we are. But these countries have one thing we don't – OIL.

As Officer Jones turned to head north on his patrol route, he noticed a new inhabitant on the southeast corner near the White House tonight. He was your typical bum. Who was this new guy before he joined the masses on the street, Officer Jones allowed his thoughts to ponder? Maybe the guy lost his job in the economic downturn, maybe the poor guy had a drug problem, or maybe the guy just loved living on the street. Hell, Officer Jones thought to himself, "I don't care!" It was twenty-eight degrees outside, my shift is almost over.

Fortunately for this poor bastard Officer Jones thought, someone or some agency, with the assistance from my hard-earned tax dollars, provided the guy with a large overcoat thick enough to help fend off the D.C. chill. Hey, I've got my own problems to deal with he thought to himself as he drove on through the snow. Early in the day, Officer Jones discovered his eldest son was in trouble. The thing about kids today is that the system had taught them better than any generation before them on how to hide and masquerade as something that you are not. His son obviously had been hanging with the wrong folks in his spare time. The District's police had arrested his son last night while riding in the car with known drug dealers. Officer Jones knew the kids from his child's youth. The other two kids in the car had been identified years before by the parents in their neighborhood as those likely to grow up to be inhabitants of the country's prison system. Instead of taking action to prevent this from happening, none of the people living in their neighborhood had taken the chance to become a positive factor in these kids' life. Even Officer Jones turned his back on the two and told his son just to steer clear. But now it was obvious his son had not steered clear, and he hoped the charges would be dropped. Officer Jones thought, just how one could explain the gun and the one pound of pure cocaine found in the car's trunk. Yes, he knew he had problems and his wife would not let him rest until he had exhausted all of his contacts on the force. Shit, Kids, and Life. It really sucked for the guys caught in the middle, he thought.

But, the guy on the corner was not homeless, nor was he alone. Three of his associates were in position on opposite street corners on Pennsylvania and Executive Avenues surrounding this house, this place that directed the war on their homeland. This place protected the family and surrogates of the soldiers who had attacked their families without provocation. Each man carried a rocket-propelled grenade launcher and several rounds under the massive coat he wore.

Tariz knew the planting and the overgrowth of the massive oak trees on the grounds of the White House were by design. Not only did they prevent too much gawking from the crowds, they prevented clear-sight attacks from persons like him. He knew that when the signal was given his team would need to act fast. He and another member of the team would fire their shots from the vantage point on Pennsylvania Avenue. The distance he knew all too well. It was a mere 107 yards from where he stood to the office of the leader of the infidels. He knew their missiles would cover this short distant in no time.

The other members of the team would have a harder task. They would fire their shots from Executive Avenue, directly in the clearance between the oak trees. This shot, was some 265 yards, but again, if the shots got off, they would hit the massive building. Besides, the destruction of the building was not their intent; letting the Americans know that their country's protective systems had broken down was. The erosion of their leaders' ability to protect the nation had resulted from one of the worst of the seven deadly sins – Greed.

Had Officer Jones driven the entire block that evening as he usually did, he would have noticed four new beggars there, all wearing similar clothing; but he veered off course to proceed home with all due speed to deal with the issues of his son's bad decision.

As each man took up his station at a corner of the great house, they

thought of their future in martyrdom. Yes, their training for the

day had led them here. Yes, they would strike a chilling blow to

America. The signal would come, they each would act, and

America would feel the fear of being vulnerable.

And if they were lucky, maybe the leader of the infidels

would be looking out of a window when the strike came. But

Allah did not teach "luck." Allah taught that every outcome was

meant to happen. And so would their strike on the White House.

It was meant to be. The wait would be short, very short, now. As

Tariz waited for the signal, he allowed himself to wonder what else

Allah had in store for this country of infidels.

Tariz had been chosen to lead this important attack. Years

before, he had lost his entire family to an Israeli bomb. Israel had

thought his parents' apartment building was a haven for extremists.

Unfortunately for Tariz's family, this information was wrong. But

many times this happened in his homeland. The international

media always called it another successful interdiction strike by the

Israeli Defense Forces. Like the American media, the Israeli media infrastructure was well trained to spin every minute detail of activities within its borders. So many times, Tariz had seen innocent Palestinians die at the hands of the American puppets in the Mideast.

After his family's death, Tariz was adopted by a great uncle who had at the core of his belief that all non-believers were to be removed from the face of the earth by any means necessary. He raised the young Tariz in a strict home where religion was the central and most important aspect of one's being. Tariz grew to believe in the extreme side of Islam and soon caught the eye of the movement's leaders. As the attacks by Israel grew stronger, more Palestinians were killed. Even after Israel had publicly stated that it would only respond to attacks, the truth was that, Israel itself was behind many of those attacks. It was known deep inside the American Intelligence structure that Israel would sacrifice its own in order to move the country's strategic goals forward. Many Israeli citizens had died at the hands of Israelis, only to have the media spin this as another attack by the extreme Islamic front that wanted no more than to have every Israeli killed.

Tariz was a physically imposing person with the intelligence to match. Many times he had used his wit instead of his muscle to out-duel an opponent. His patience and ability to use his mind soon pushed him into the forefront of the movement's leadership.

Tariz knew his long wait to strike a major blow to the heart of the infidels would soon be over. He had trained for this moment. He had been allowed to hand-pick his team and had chosen men he knew. Each of them had lost someone to the infidels. The Infidels had easily dispensed death on others.

Now with one pull of Tariz's finger, the throne of the infidels would at last know the fear his homeland had known for years. The Infidels would have to live with the fear of not knowing when a missile, bomb, or poison would end the flame of life. Tariz was ready. He was confident –he knew with every ounce of his belief in Allah that each member of his team would respond once the signal was received.

Chapter 8 - Lost

Robert needed the money. He was on the verge of being evicted from his four-hundred-dollar-a-month apartment. His addiction to drugs, alcohol and sex had caused him to lose his family and the support of his friends. Earlier Robert had spoken to his mom, who always wanted better for her son. But she knew her failed marriage, the bitter fights in front of Robert, and the eventual death of his father due to a life-long battle with alcoholism doomed her son to the life he now lived.

She had told her son, "Robert I always loved you and will continue to love you. I am sorry for the home in which you were raised and if I could turn back the hands of time, I would do anything so I could have a second chance to give you a loving home environment." Robert welcomed the warmth from his mother but could not or would not absorb the affection. As he knew and remembered only a painful past, he could not fully appreciate the love his mother offered to him.

He had been told many times not to leave the keys of his company's delivery van inside the unlocked vehicle. Therefore, he should not have been surprised when the vehicle was not in its usual spot when he awoke the next morning. Fearing more trouble, he decided not to report the truck stolen so he did not report to work. Knowing it took county government several days to process termination papers, he thought he would at least attempt to find the truck before going back to work to be fired. He started out by canvassing his neighborhood, thinking some of the kids had taken it for a joy ride.

He checked all the usual places. He had walked five blocks when he ran into several friends. As usual, they were on their way to the local tavern to have their mid-day lunch drinks. Hell, Robert thought to himself, I'll go back to look for the truck after hanging out with the guys. After several hours of drinking and talking a lot about a little, Robert left the tavern to continue his search. The alcohol gave him a false sense of protection against the cold weather and had Robert known the plot unfolding just blocks away from him on Pennsylvania Avenue his high might've melted as fast as a snowball in a blast furnace.

His truck was only three blocks from the tavern, hidden in a brownstone's garage. That day the truck would carry its most important load, one thousand pounds of high explosives, all gathered by Tariz and friends from the infidel's unprotected construction sites. The believers in Allah who were carrying out this most important task thought the people of this country were arrogant. How could they kill, steal and consume the economies of weaker nations, damage people's beliefs and thus change the outcomes of faith through their notion that the American way was the only way?

Today to answer those questions by their deeds, he and his fellow believers would continue what had begun on September 11, 2001. Today they would strike a blow to the heart of the lion. Today's attacks would exceed the damage done on that fateful day in 2001. September 11, 2001, brought 3,000 deaths this country of unbelievers and had quickly been forgotten. After spending billions on the Homeland Security Plan, it was still easy for enemies to move within the borders of the great American beast. A body as big as America had too many openings to secure. The believers of Allah had learned much from 9-11. On that day, many had died, and many died months later from the lung diseases and cancer caused by inhaling the dust from the Twin Towers' collapse. But since Americans believed more in amassing paper with the pictures of dead presidents on it; dollar bills, than in a higher Being, they moved on easily after the deaths.

The faithful had learned that fear stops with death. But with life, fear continues once it becomes part of the daily fabric. Fear, not death, is the virus of the capitalist. Fear will make a worker afraid of showing up to work; death will insure the work doesn't get done. But the dead worker can be replaced, whereas the scared worker only spreads fear to his coworkers, which makes the problem worse for the capitalist.

Like the H1N1 virus that spread from Mexico across the globe, the terrorists had mutated to become virus-like. The terrorists changed its form to meet the conditions of the host so that when necessary an appropriately deadly blow could be delivered. However, Tariz knew it was not the death they would bring, but the virus of fear that would spread throughout this so-called great country that would eventually bring it to its knees. Yes, fear, not death, had become the ultimate weapon against the U.S. With the citizens of the country being fearful of the next bomb and next event, they would slow their productivity, slow their innovation and not perform at a level needed to sustain the great American economic engine.

Once this happened, America would no longer be in a position to project its strength across the globe. He and his countrymen would not repeat the mistake of the Japanese when they attacked Pearl Harbor. Had the Japanese followed up their air strike with more strikes and a land invasion, the outcome of the War would have been different. Unknown to the Japanese their first strike had struck a severe blow to the Americans. A second attack and a follow-up land invasion could have given the Japanese a beachhead on American territory and would have placed fear directly in the lives of millions of west-coast Americans.

This snowy day, the bomb was ready. He and his cell would simply await the signal.

The traffic engineer was sure he had entered the correct code. The traffic control computer system was a new multi-million dollar system purchased to heighten national security after 9-11. The grant to obtain the money from the 9-11 security funds was based on the critical need to move traffic in and out of the District during periods of national crisis. Over the past several days, several bugs had been uncovered in the new software update. The new code would ease traffic congestion on many of the busier intercity corridors. The goal was to assure that workers got in on time and later were able to exit the city as fast as possible.

The system used cameras, and unknown to the drivers of the new cars with the "Global Positioning Satellite" systems, the global positioning systems locators allowed traffic engineers to track individuals and their habits. These variables were fed into the super-computer, which calculated the load on the streets and the timing needed by the traffic signals to increase flow. The system analyzed multiple factors and utilized this data to make minute changes to the Districts' signals. The result was on-time demand-control of traffic signals so that inflow and outflow into the District flowed as well as an orchestrated concert.

Today, the traffic engineer finally put his ego on the sideline and dialed the 800 number to the software vendor for assistance. As with most 800 numbers in America, the call was not sent to an American-based help desk. Ironically, the person on the other end of the line was actually located in Saudi Arabia. The contractor had trained all of their account representatives well.

The English and history classes combined with a well-placed understanding of the traffic control software program would lead any person seeking help to think they were talking with any Billy or Betty Ann from Nebraska.

Today the help-desk attendant would solve the traffic engineer's problem. As with most software packages, programmers included a backdoor applet to allow help-desk personnel to take control of the application in order to fix problems. With a few keystrokes and the assistance of the Internet, the Saudi help-desk attendant had logged into the District of Columbia's traffic control computer. Once he was in, he quickly scanned the system for bugs. He spotted the problem and within five minutes had logged off and informed the DC traffic engineer what had caused the problem. After accepting the DC traffic engineer's thanks the call ended. Unknown to the American, the Saudi help desk attendant had left a little present in the software code he had just uploaded to the District's new traffic control system. At precisely eight p.m. all of the District's traffic lights changed to red for ten seconds. Fortunately, due to the cold weather, traffic inside the beltline was light. After the brief incident, the traffic lights went back to normal. Slightly amused, the night attendant at the District of Columbia's traffic control center logged this anomaly for the daytime manager to review and to decide whether further action was needed.

Chapter 9 – Cross Roads

Zachary's trip to Camp Pendleton in California was another expenditure of valuable time he didn't have much of and it didn't help it had rained for most of the trip. He had put off his trip for several weeks, attempting to track the terrorist suspects associated with Scarlet Badge.

The research team at Camp Pendleton needed him to review the new technology being developed for his counter-espionage teams. The equipment, Zachary knew, would save lives. But it would still be months before his guys would gain access to it. Field tests would be needed and more money allocated by Congress in order to outfit all of the teams with the goods.

The day had gone fast and Zachary was happy for that. He had rented a convertible for a quick trip north to Los Angeles. Several of his childhood friends had moved there and he would use his downtime to make a visit. He was not due back home until Monday, and Karla was okay with him spending some time with his friends, several of whom he hadn't seen for more than a decade. The drive up Interstate 5 was enjoyable. Traveling at eighty-five miles per hour, some twenty miles over the speed limit with the wind in your hair, was definitely a relaxing escape.

As soon as he cleared the next rise in the road, he saw what he did not want to see. Yes, the California Highway Patrol he had grown up watching on television was now a growing image in his rear-view mirror. Well, he would need to explain this one to the guy behind the Camaro's wheel, speeding twenty miles above the posted speed limit. As Zachary pulled his car over on the dry, sandy shoulder, he took out his license, military identification, and rental car registration. He also instinctively placed his hands back on the steering wheel to show the officer he meant him no ill will. California was a locus of high patrolman anxiety, given the recent rash of shootings and chases resulting in the death and injury of several officers. As the officer approached from the driver's side of the car, Zachary could see he had his hands at the ready to pull his service revolver. He asked Zachary, "Sir, I need your license and registration and why were you in such a hurry?" "I am headed to Los Angeles to see an old friend," Zachary responded. The officer sarcastically replied, "Well I guess your friend will have to wait while we handle this problem, now won't he?"

The officer informed Zachary of the California law stating anyone driving twenty miles or more over the posted speed limit could lose their license, then he walked back to his patrol car.

Zachary knew that if the officer escalated this situation, all he had to do was to make a phone call to his commanding officer and this problem would be erased as if someone had blotted it out with a large bottle of whiteout.

As the officer returned with Zachary's information in tow, Zachary saw he did not have the pink citation in hand. "Sir, I noticed you serve in the Special Forces Unit. I also served in the army before I was discharged several years ago. We are definitely in a different era now and I commend you and thank you for the job you are doing to protect me, my family and this country." Zachary replied, "No kidding. We are definitely in a fight with an enemy that is not easily identified. Hell, your own neighbor could now be the enemy." They both agreed that America was now open to attack from people who did not care about the true history and values of the country. The officer asked Zachary what he would do if he ever came face to face with any enemy within the borders of the United States. Zachary did not hesitate: "I would kill them"

He replied. The officer nodded in agreement as he waved Zachary Wilson back onto I-5. That afternoon after his shift ended, the officer went to the local military base and reenlisted in the reserves as he instinctively knew a war would soon rage here, and he too wanted to be one of America's defenders.

In Los Angeles, Zachary called his friend Richard. Richard was an ex-Army Ranger who had done his twenty years and gotten out. Richard had retired from the military and entered civilian life as a contractor for a security firm. His skills developed from the many years in the green jungles of the world prepared him for his new role as a designer of systems to eliminate problems caused by the animals in America's concrete jungle.

Zachary was happy to see that his old friend had a few cold ones in the refrigerator. The drive up in the open air had dried him out. Zachary and Richard quickly caught up on each other's activities and their families. Zachary asked, "How is your cousin Greg doing?" Greg was one heck of an athlete. He was definitely the best out of the bunch from their childhood gang. He could throw the football a country mile, hit the baseball like Hank Aaron, and would run over would-be tacklers like Jim Brown. Richard yelled from his bedroom, "Greg has found Christ, has two children and is living a peaceful life in their old hometown." Zachary felt sorry for Richard as he knew the military had robbed yet another man of the opportunity to have a meaningful family life. Richard's family for twenty years had been the men who followed him into battle. These had been his sons and nephews. His wife had been the jungles of the world. After this, he had traded the life of a successful military man for the life of a lonely one. But Richard did not show the effects of being lonely. His job kept him busy and his involvement in the local community helping disadvantaged children and their families obtain healthcare services kept him busy. Knowing the wastage in the federal and state systems, he could not understand why people had to forego health care as a result of a lack of financial resources.

Zachary and Richard hung around Richard's home discussing old times. Zachary asked, "Man do you remember the time you, me and Fat-Cat set the woods behind my parents' house on fire? We burned down the straw hut our gang built." Richard replied, Yeah I remember, it was a cold winter day and we decided to build a fire inside a straw hut. How smart was that?" Zachary said, "Man we and the rest of our friends put a lot of time into building that hut. It had three rooms and enough room to hold eight of us at one time. The rest of our gang was pissed when they found out we burned it down." Richard responded, "Yeah we would have burned the woods down if it hadn't been for Greg. As I recall he was always saving our behinds from something." Both laughed at that statement as Greg was the group's defender from all outside threats.

Both agreed, those days back in their hometown were the good old days. Long hot days of meeting early in the morning after breakfast to roam free without the concerns of today's child or their parents who now must be on constant watch for people intent on causing harm. The good old days allowed a child to grow to understand the true essence of a community. In those days, not only did you have your family, but also your community was your extended family. You knew the folks on your block had your back, and your parents knew this was the case. Kids played in each others' back yards without the slightest frown from the owner of the yard concerned about his or her fescue. Kids were allowed to cut through yards on their bikes. Kids were allowed to play basketball at someone's house even if the owners were not home. You didn't need a vet to house your dog when you went away, because you knew a neighbor would water and feed your dog.

The day the hut caught on fire, cousin Greg put out the fire by fanning and smothering the flames with an old blanket. As quickly as it started, it was over and their fears were allayed. The boys gathered in one of the neighborhood backyards and played a game of pickup football. As it was, those indeed were the good old days when boys managed to set their natural misdeeds to rights, felt good about it, and then forgot about it.

Zachary and Richard decided to get something to eat at the local mall. Zachary wanted to hit some of the local nightclubs and he needed to buy an outfit for the night's events. The old friends headed for the Outback Steakhouse at the mall.

Although he was a Muslim, his appetite for Western food sometimes caused Abdul to stray from his religion's dietary guidelines. The day had been a good one. He sold four cars and wanted to celebrate with his wife and child. He called Christina and asked her to meet him at the local Outback. He planned to buy his wife and child a gift at the mall once they finished eating.

Zachary and Richard were in a booth near the bar so they could watch ESPN while they talked. Many wives did not understand the communication between men. They could sit in the same room without uttering a word and still seem to have a conversation. Women, on the other hand, had to talk.

Abdul was happy to see Christina and Malik arrive and gave them a huge hug. He asked, both of them, "How was your day and how was the drive to the restaurant?" Christina replied, "We had a wonderful day and your little ball of energy kept me company all day long". Christina and Abdul were doubly happy to know the wait tonight was only five minutes. The hostess seated the family next to Zachary and Richard. As both groups discussed the day's events and plans for the evening, they gave each a quick glance and continued their dining. Abdul told his wife, "I sold four cars today! My manager gave me a $100 gift card to this restaurant and told me to have a great evening with my family." Abdul told his wife as his son listened intently, "The continued escalation in gas prices and loss of jobs were forcing more and more Americans to opt for used cars that achieved high gas mileage rates and that were cheaper than a brand new car. He told her his boss had told the team although this was good for used car dealerships in the short term, it could pose a major problem in the long term as more and more American's lost their jobs and remained unemployed for longer periods of time." Abdul knew that no job meant no money and no money meant a person could not buy a car or anything else. As they waited for their food, both groups of family and friends enjoyed catching up and discussing the news of the day.

Christina al-Kariim was happy to see her husband in such a good mood. She truly loved him and respected him dearly. He had sacrificed much for her happiness, and for this she would give her life if asked. Abdul could see the admiration in his wife's eyes. And his son was truly a jewel produced from their bodies some years ago. Yes, just like the pressure and heat of the earth-produced diamonds in Africa, their heat and pressure from the love their relationship built had also produced a jewel, their jewel – Malik. Malik was busy coloring with the free crayons and paper activity book provided the hostess. Abdul thought briefly that this restaurant was truly a friend of the parents, keeping the child busy while allowing parents to relax, on top of providing a good square and tasty meal.

Abdul told Christina, "I spoke with my friend Mashir today. He stopped by the dealership. He wanted to catch me up on his recent visit to Afghanistan." Abdul continued, "Mashir told me things were not good in our homeland. He said many children were starving and the elderly were left to fend for themselves." Abdul told Christina, "Mashir and many others of the true followers are angry because the puppet leader installed by the infidels' was doing nothing to improve the situation." However, Abdul instinctively knew the situation was complicated by tribal chiefdoms that actually ran things in the country outside of Kabul.

He told his wife, "It was unfortunate his home country would never be more than a crossroads between the West and East. Marco Polo and others had traveled here only to find it to be a barren wasteland of mountains dotted with beautiful valleys. The valleys were in short supply but were fertile. This fact had not escaped the local drug traffickers who grew poppy plants there to harvest the opium from the processing of the seeds." Mashir, Abdul continued, "Discussed his desire to move his mother and father maybe to England where his younger brother was in school." Like any child, Abdul told Christina, "Mashir wanted to know his parents were able to live their last days in this world in peace and satisfaction. He had seen the economic conditions in his country steadily lower his parents' standard of living. But he also knew that at this point in their lives, uprooting them would probably be harder on them than allowing them to stay. He had taken all of the necessary steps so that after he entered Paradise, his family and siblings would be taken care of for eternity."

Abdul, as Christina knew, was a person with a keen sense of perception. Something about his friend didn't seem right. A person who knows there is no escaping death, faces death with peace. This same person also approaches life differently from a person who is attempting to live. A person that is attempting to defy death is paranoid and schizophrenic, trying by any means necessary to cheat death of its quarry. The best a person can do is to delay the eventuality that death will always win. No matter what is done, death will seep into one's life, stealing the daylight and replacing it with eternal darkness.

Abdul told his wife, "Honey, I am really troubled because Mashir seems at peace with himself and I feel does not care if he lives or dies." He continued, "My gut is telling something is going own, something is being planned and since Mashir's return from our homeland, he has changed his outlook on life." Christina asked, "What do you think is going on with your friend. You don't think he is planning to do anything drastic do you?" She looked and her husband and asked, "Really honey, I don't know him well, but you don't think he's involved in any of this kill American stuff because America is a bad country do you? Come on, if America is so bad, why in the heck do so many people try to get here?" Abdul's sixth sense that told him something was underway and his friend was in the middle of it. Being in the middle had caused his friend to accept his faith, and this caused chill bumps to run down Abdul's spine. At this moment he knew, he knew what he did not know, but he knew what would come and he wanted no part of it. Yes, today had been sunny and beautiful, but at this moment the night had stolen the beauty of the day, replacing it with the dark of the night. Those who sought death would steal life's glow soon.

To change the subject, Abdul asked his son, "Hey Malik what are you coloring?"

The discussion at the table to his right did not escape Zachary's keen ears. Although he wore glasses, actually since twelfth grade in high school, he was blessed with good hearing. He surmised the good Lord did not want to have a soldier in the U.S. military running through the jungles and trouble spots of the world both blind and deaf. Richard saw the change on his old friend's face. Richard was discussing the plans for tonight, but he could see his old friend was not listening. He was processing other data. Zachary's eyes locked in on Richard's and he could see Zachary was making decisions. Zachary Wilson was transforming back into the warrior soldier. Something had triggered this in him and Richard allowed the process to continue.

To the untrained, the conversation between the Caucasian woman, Middle Eastern man, and mixed-race child would seem normal, a man telling his wife about a troubled friend. This was typical, given the number of Americans hurting from the 2008 economic downturn that eroded the quality and standard of living for so many. But, was this just an innocent conversation? Did it mean more? He asked his friend Richard if he knew where the mosque the man mentioned was located. "I do and we'll actually go near it tonight on our way to the club I want to take you to", Richard replied.

"Excellent," Zachary marveled. He excused himself from the table and went outside to make a call. Yes, Zachary Wilson was in work mode tonight. He pulled out his micro-sized satellite phone and made a call to the night watchman. "Lieutenant, I need you to run some data points on the mosque. Please reread the address I gave to you to verify you have the correct information, Zachary asked. "Please call me as soon as you have something of interest." "Yes, Sir", the Lieutenant responded.

When he returned to the table he saw his food was there. Good timing! He didn't know how much longer his stomach could take just grinding air. Zachary continued to listen in on the adjacent table's small talk. Dinner went quickly as the friends knew the night was going to be interesting, especially if hostiles were discovered and they needed occurred to eradicate them. After dinner, Richard and Zachary sat in the car until they saw the young family leaving the restaurant. The young boy reminded

Zachary so much of his own children. He bounced ahead of his parents to their car, where he was strapped into his car seat. Zachary and Richard could see the young Arab truly loved and cared for his family. Zachary wondered whether this guy represented a threat or not. If it was determined he did, another single parent family would soon be created.

The attack on the homeland on September 11, 2001 clearly changed the rules of engagement. A threat to the country even by people who called America home had to be stamped out of existence. Like a fly uninvited to a cookout, terrorists would be swatted away with the unbridled force of the persons assigned to protecting the American people. Zachary thought briefly of his family, especially his children, and hoped he would not have to make this woman the sole provider for this beautiful and innocent child.

After obtaining the license tag of the vehicle, Zachary re-keyed the number to the night watch station and soon had the home address, occupation, and other relevant information on the persons in the car, which had just driven off. The occupants were indeed married, and the husband sold cars for a living. They had only one child, and the young Arab had attended school in the United States, primarily in California. The other information provided was basic, a few misdeeds in college but nothing to raise alarm bells. Zachary could see that he was also a long-term member of the mosque he and Richard would soon drive by, but this association did not make him an immediate threat. Maybe a person of interest, but not yet a threat. If the latter were determined, it would only be for a short period of time, Zachary surmised, as he adjusted his gun's shoulder harness.

As Richard turned the corner in downtown Los Angeles, Zachary quickly made out the target. Most mosques, especially those of rich Muslims were well appointed. In this town with its large Arab population, mosques dotted the landscape like cactuses in the desert. Conveniently, placed where members of the Muslim religion could express their dedication to Allah, some mosques had become bastions of hatred. Whether it was right-winged Christians, Protestants or militant Arabs, it was wrong to use religion as a basis for hate, Zachary thought.

Zachary Carson Wilson was a simple animal. He attempted to break the complexities in his life down into simple components.

Through this process, he could maintain a sense of control. Most religions view life as a time in which to praise and thank God and to help and express love for themselves and others. But when a religion allows extremism and absolutism to enter its doors, the house of worship becomes a breeding ground of hate that develops into a belief system aimed at destroying others in the name of that religion's Almighty or god, Zachary mused. Whether it was the Pilgrims and the Indians or the Spanish and the South American Indian, or the Jew against the Arab, those set on conquering another have always used their religion as the final approval for attacking another, Zachary thought. This type of belief has no limits when the person has crossed the line into extremism, when one believes that causing death is acceptable to one's God. Zachary thought to himself, "there is indeed is a thin line between love and hate."

He keyed further information into the satellite phone, and then he looked at his old friend. The look on his face told Richard everything he needed to know. Death would soon fly through the open night sky with the unabated freedom of a prehistoric river. Riding this river's crest would be Zachary Wilson! The sandbars and logs that attempted to dam its progress would be washed away and into the abyss of eternal darkness.

Zachary quickly saw he was getting too old for the nightclub scene. Richard, "You know I never enjoyed dancing. Man, even when we went to the local dances in the parking lot at our high school, I didn't dance." "I also hate these crowds now", he quipped. Richard replied, "Brother, just relax your mind and try to enjoy this momentary break from your worries." In addition Richard knew his old friend was not Fred Astaire on the dance floor, either!

Zachary told Richard, "Los Angeles women are beautiful, but the most beautiful women are found only in Miami." Richard said they would need to figure out how they could work out a road trip to Miami to allow him to see first-hand this gold mine of women Zachary described.

The men relaxed as they took in a few good drinks. Zachary was glad to see the bartender did not water down the content of alcohol in his favorite drink, Long Island Iced Tea. He had come to favor this drink in college. The local dance club on his campus made these drinks in large glasses for an inexpensive price. The buzz came quickly and prevented one from going broke from having to purchase too many drinks.

As Zachary watched the L.A. youth mill about in the nightclub, he thought how fortunate he was to be married. No longer having the need to go out weekly to impress someone or reeducate someone else on who and what he stood for. The nice thing about being married was that the woman who had pledged herself to you and you to her, knew exactly who it was they woke up beside each morning -- well almost every morning if you were able to keep yourself out of the dog house. Anyway, a married man could count on dealing for the majority of time with the known. For a man like Zachary, the known had to be flushed out, because he feared the unknown. Failure to uncover the unknowns could mean death for the unsuspecting.

After several hours of club hopping, the friends decided to end the night at a local breakfast eatery near Richard's home. Zachary got his favorite, waffles topped with whipped cream and strawberries, sausage and cheese eggs, with a side of toast and jelly. Richard said, "Man how in the world can you eat so much and remain fit? You did the same thing when we were kids. Any time I came to your house, I knew I better get all of the food your mom offered on the first round, because you and your brothers didn't leave anything for seconds." Zachary told his friend, "Hey, I only eat this way on special occasions now and with this high cholesterol I have to watch my intake of foods high in fat." He continued, "American's food industry is in partnership with the drug industry anyway, hell one gives us bad food to and the other gives us drugs that only prolong life, but never cures anything. That way both industries have access to a market continually in need of their services." Zachary quietly allowed himself to think about his mom. Her final years on earth were negatively affected by diabetes and Alzheimer's. He wondered how much of her health problems were caused by bad food and ineffectual medications.

The next morning Zachary arose early to make plans to return to base. The day would be full of activities, some new to the agenda. The information provided from last night's excursion turned up some interesting facts. Maybe I should go out to clubs more, he thought to himself. First, the mosque had become a center of radical anti-Americanism. The mosque's Inman was long-time member on the FBI's watch list. Over the past several months, the level of extremism there had increased. The local FBI office had been successful in inserting counter-intelligence assets into the mosque. The information to this point had not been shared with the military, a problem still present throughout the intelligence establishment even after the post 9-11 reforms were enacted, because political appointees were still placing the importance of putting feathers in their individual hats above the safety of the American people. They also were scrupulous in following the Bill of Rights.

But, the undercover agents at the mosque were providing invaluable information. Although the information was not specific to an attack, it did lead the directors of the many joint agencies to increase their scrutiny of the information generated. Yes, something was going to happen, but the available information was not conclusive enough and could not be used to develop solutions to the potential problems.

Zachary's drive back to base was enjoyable. The convertible allowed the Pacific breeze to flow over him. The air reminded him of the breezy days back in his childhood home. No threats, no pain, no death, his childhood home, though rural, was a place of peace. The Pacific breeze did not smell like the air of his childhood, but the salt air caused him to daydream as he drove. The fall seasons of his youth were the best times of the year in his hometown. He thought about the smell of pine straw burning, the seasonable nights, and the walks to his high school to watch the Friday night football games. Yes, life was simple and it was good back then. He and his friends had wished for the days of adulthood and back then it really puzzled Zachary and his friends why the adults around them always wished for the days of their youth. Now he understood fully! He had been insulated against the true nature of the world -- a place of death and mayhem. The world needed someone like him to eradicate problems so more could know the peaceful life of his childhood. Zachary knew this was his place in life, and he had been given the skills to perform this task. He would not waste this talent. He felt the time was coming soon when his talents would be needed and displayed on a grand scale.

As he entered his office, desk clerk gave him a note from his Commanding Officer. Scarlet Badge was on the move. His team's ability to track the Internet chatter and other communications of Scarlet Badge had gotten better. Due to a slip-up uncovered three months ago when Scarlet Badge assets were communicating about training activities in Pakistan, America's intelligence network had caught a limited amount of a transmission that indicated one of Scarlet Badge's main assets had left the United States for a long-planned stay in a near-east country.

Zachary's team was hot on the trail of any connections to Scarlet Badge in the continental United States. So, had it not been for an overzealous co-worker who thought it would be amusing to report a former co-worker as a potential terrorist just because he had left his company without notice, and had it not been for the junior FBI watch agent receiving the information, the connection to Youssef Aziz might have never been made.

Zachary's team had been working overtime to determine who Youssef Aziz was. They had learned that Aziz was a person who had achieved all of the things any American wanted, plenty of money, many tangible assets and the power to go along with it. His recent failure to receive the CEO's position in his company had resulted in his leaving the country with his entire family in tow.

That was strangely extreme behavior the team felt. Recent

information pointing towards potential attacks on America's

infrastructure made him a potential target for Zachary's team.

Zachary contacted his team's intelligence office. He asked

the duty officer, "Do you have any updates on this new target?"

The duty officer could hear the intensity in the Zachary's voice.

The duty officer told Zachary, "No sir, we have all of our

intelligence assets targeted on this individual Aziz. We have

developed an overview of his background, but we have not

connected him to any groups that we were recently following."

The duty officer continued, "We are conducting forensic analyses

of his banking, trading and other financial activities and should

have those ready for presentation within 48 hours." The duty

officer assured Zachary, "If this guy Youssef Aziz had any dirt on

him, they would definitely uncover it. Since 9-11, agencies can no

longer hide behind their false fences of agency autonomy.

Taxpayers have funded, vast computer networks had been linked

together to allow those with access to mine their data. Slow speed

is the only problem with doing this as was having the computer

system with the ability to do the data mining quickly", the duty officer concluded. Zachary told the Information Officer. "Well, please proceed as quickly as you can!" "Something in the back of my mind is telling me we are on to something big", he told the duty officer. Instinctively, he also knew these things take time to build out. "Thank you for all of your help", he told the duty officer. "Yes sir," quipped the duty officer.

Zachary's flight home was due to leave at noon. This would put him back on the East Coast by 6:00 p.m. The nice thing about where he and Karla had chosen to live was that it was only fifteen minutes from the airport. He did not have to worry about long drives or traffic jams on the commute home from the airport. During the flight, Zachary thought about the events that had unfolded on this trip.

He wondered if this Youssef fellow was indeed a dot to be connected in the larger matrix of what he and his team were working on. If he was, then he hoped that it would be discovered in good time. But Zachary knew that neither time nor the decision of when things happened in time was in his control. It was truly unfortunate that his team could not act on suspicion. If this were the old Soviet Union or Communist China, Youssef unknown to his family and close associates would have been picked up in his new homeland and brought back to the United States for interrogation.

But the United States followed a set of rules established by men who wanted to ensure an orderly pattern to war and peace. However, these rules were written during the 1780's when countries and men at war lacked the technology for people to attach bombs to themselves and kill innocent civilians or to fly jumbo jets into buildings. Yes, this was a new era; and to fight this subtle new enemy, America needed a new set of rules of engagement.

The new rules would not be set by the current administration nor the guys and gals in Congress. Protecting civil liberties was paramount for Congress in order, to ensure the Constitution's integrity -- Zachary Wilson knew this. America was a fragile state. America's fragile state of existence was maintained only by the belief of those Americans whose families had been here long enough to understand what true freedom meant. As more and more individuals migrated here from countries less open, Zachary knew over time, the open society he and his ancestors had grown to expect could easily become closed. This assessment was based on the fact that America was a democracy governed by the majority. Americans descended from persons born in this country were becoming less a percent of the country's total population.

This erosion in the majority would eventually lead to the birth of new thoughts and beliefs showing up in the policies enacted by Congress. Zachary thought how a virus invaded a body not by frontal attack but slowly through gaps in the body's armor. So too was America being invaded slowly by persons who did not believe in his country's Constitution. Zachary instinctively knew the new war would be fought on his homeland and he wanted to be like the human body's front line of defense – the white blood cells. The battlefield was his home, not sitting behind some desk trying to figure out subplots being developed by terrorists.

Zachary's plane landed fifteen minutes early due to a kind west to east tail wind that gave the jumbo jet an extra boost. Ten minutes after that, he was in his car heading home to his wife and children. When he pulled up in the yard, he could see Kristen; his little daughter, standing in the front window looking out for her father. She opened the door and ran out and gave him a huge hug.

Zachary thought, it's the littlest people who give the greatest love. A child knows no enemy at his daughter's age, and the internal flame burning inside him would ensure she never was confronted with someone whom she would need to call her enemy. As long as blood flowed through his veins, Zachary Carson Wilson would be her protector.

Thus, he needed to find out more about the Youssef fellow. Zachary knew that by now, the fellow at the restaurant would have had his phones bugged and every moved watched. The nice thing about the new homeland security rules was the ease of obtaining wiretap approval and other counter surveillance initiatives. Hell, Zachary chuckled as he hugged his daughter; approvals for wiretaps from judges were no longer needed. Yes, 9-11 had opened up a few freedoms for those assigned to protecting the masses, although there would be hell to pay if this new tactic ever became public.

Zachary walked into the house and heard his boys upstairs; yes, indeed, he was home, and happy that he was. Zachary yelled out, "Hey, your daddy is home, come show me some love." Although he knew his sons loved him, they were at the age where they saw their father as an enforcer of the rules and the border at the extension of their freedoms. They knew to cross the borders would be to enter into a minefield from which they would not return unscathed. Inside these borders the rules of the country called Karla reigned supreme. Zachary's sons; Keith and Drew, each had learned these fine details as they grew into their early teen years. Karla's rules were stringent but were fair. So were Zachary's laws that covered extra-border activities. Yes the boys had learned well and early and therefore there had been very few times Zachary had instituted his rules of capital punishment, which was fine by him.

His sons finally made it downstairs and both at the same time as if they had practiced, it jointly said, "Hey dad, how was the trip? Did you get a chance to check on the new video game for the Play Station?" Zachary knew the drill, the boys showed up and after he tossed them the new video game quickly disappeared back to their territory -- the game room. On their way out of the living room, the duet in sync said, "Thanks Dad." Karla came out from the office and gave her husband a hug and began to tell him about all the events that had unfolded on her job and in the neighborhood. "Do you believe they are threatening to lay off key project staff? All of those managers who sit back in their offices and wait for us to give them the finalized reports that they then take and present as their own work it just ridiculous." "By the way, the houses down the street finally sold and the new families each have little girls Kristen's age. The neighborhood is turning in a play land for girls." Zachary, knowing this was part of the welcome-home party, sat and listened intently, although his thoughts were elsewhere. He had learned how to look attentive even though his mind was processing information that he hoped would keep his family and those around him safe.

Zachary's obvious pretense placed significant strain in the family as Karla felt she was a secondary concern to Zachary's career. Additionally, Karla was always complaining about Zachary making plans with his brothers to plan events for the kids. The smallest discussion with his brother about getting the kids together with their grandfather caused a Karla outbreak. These observations had pushed her to feel the need to take more control of her life. So Karla's drive to take control and Zachary's failure to be more of a listener drove a wedge between them. Only through their tenacity was the family kept together as a unit. With a husband and wife of lesser character, the family was often torn apart by divorce.

Hell, he smiled as he thought; Karla would make one hell of a foot soldier in my unit and would definitely impale the enemy with her sharp sword, if only she would listen to his orders and logic, two things that did not happen now. Oh well, he thought, at least she kept the family moving forward towards success. Karla had prepared a quick and easy dinner, spaghetti and salad. The kids loved the stuff and it filled them up. After dinner and cleanup, Zachary and Karla asked the kids, "Anyone want to play a quick game of Wii Mario Karts before bed time." The family all rushed upstairs to claim their spot on the game room floor where they would twist and turn and scream and shout as their Mario carts bounced and smashed each other around the television screen.

Zachary and Karla stayed awake another two hours as they caught one another up on the happenings in each one's life. Karla told Zachary, "I want to leave my job by the end of the year. I don't like it, I don't like the people I work with, because the leadership is so cut throat. I wish I could have gone onto graduate school as I had planned. I just feel my entire career has been a waste", she concluded. "I fully support any action you want to take", Zachary told his wife. "I want you to enjoy your life and do those things you enjoy. Hell, life is too short to come to the end and have regrets of what you did or didn't do" he told Karla. "The four score and ten years we are given should be used wisely and treated with care", he told his wife as he rub her back. "I want you to have the freedom to seek out any goal you have, honey. What can I do to help you?" "I will do whatever I can to give you the base, the foundation you need, but you know, my job requires me to leave on a moment's notice. I promise you that I will work hard to provide the environment you need to work on your career aspirations, but please do not ask me to curtail his level of commitment to his country at this critical point", he concluded. Karla knew Zachary had enough service years, successes and connections that would allow him to receive a nice post at the Pentagon. Why wouldn't he make this commitment to her and the children? He was away so much, despite the fact that in the grand scheme of things, Zachary was deployed less frequently now than he had ever been before. Zachary's team consisted of forty-plus men. Typically, he sent his junior officers on the long deployments in enemy territory when needed, though Zachary always went along when he knew the situation would and could be dicey. He never allowed his men to take risks he was unwilling to assume himself. The men under his command had families too.

The next morning at an early 4:30 a.m., Zachary kissed Karla on the forehead as she slept and looked in on his children before heading out to the base. He knew his professional success was linked directly to the support received from his wife although she chose to display it in a way that caused him stress. Yes, she was always there to allow him to leave on a moment's notice and yet his leaving always led to a cutting comment or an argument. Was it the fear of losing him or the hate she held against him for having chosen this career that caused her to respond the angry way she did, he thought. Oh well, like a bad radio signal received on a fisherman's radio in the wilderness fly-fishing, Zachary learned to tune out the noise.

As he drove the route to the base, he passed many other cars. Probably folks headed to their jobs, too. He wondered how many people he was passing could be potential terrorists. The problem with the new war is that we do not know who the enemy is. This new enemy has grown to hate what the country stands for and is. Many people in America do not understand the true value of the country.

The history taught to children had become less of a civics lesson on the ways America over the course of its existence had truly been the land of the free to more of a lesson on America the world's bully. These changes had occurred as more and more state and national assemblies had become more influenced by those who did not totally support America's historical values and beliefs.

He hoped for some breaks in the case as he felt something big was being planned by Scarlet Badge. Upon arriving at his office on his desk Zack saw the report with information about the mystery guy at the Outback in Los Angeles. The report on Malik al-Kariim indicated he was a hard-working used-car salesman, married and with one child, Abdul. He had worked several jobs since dropping out of college, but held the used-car salesman's job for the past three years. He married an American, lived in the same twelve-mile radius for several years, moving from apartment to apartment. It dawned on Zachary how limited the scope of life truly is when one looks at where we live, work, and shop.

There is so much to life, he thought, yet we live out our existence within an area that amounts to something the size of a needle's eye. Well, he would assign some assets to watch this guy for a few weeks to see if it anything meaningful turned up.

Things were not starting off well today. The other reports on his desk indicated the trail of Youssef Aziz had gone cold. It was just as if Aziz and his family had dropped off the face of the earth. If this were true, Zachary knew his instincts had been right. Something was up, and the something might be a major attack within America's borders.

Zachary picked up his phone and called his counterpart in England. England was still America's greatest ally, always willing to share information, unlike Russia and China. Zachary knew this came as a result of England's realization that it was only America who could come to the rescue if China decided to flex its muscle, its economic growth evident over the past decade since 2000. China was becoming a global bully, using its newfound technological advances and the fact that America was addicted to its cheap imports, to move unabated from region to region. Several months ago, China had sailed several of its blue ocean ships through the Strait of Taiwan to flex its muscle as a rival to America's naval strength in the region. Truly England needed America, and America needed England. This had always been the case and was even more of a fact now.

Zachary's old friend Colonel Turner told him their intelligence assets had picked up on voice traffic indicating something was being planned and it was big. The information did not indicate a country or time. But everyone assumed if a major attack was being planned it would be either a strike in England or America. Terrorists were not targeting Russia or China as a result of both countries becoming friendlier to the Arab world and less friendly to Israel. So there they were, two old friends with their collective backs against the world.

The situation had worsened with the American President's foreign policy strategy that alienated even those countries and groups who longed for a strong relationship with the United States. This American President was indeed a cowboy. His ill-advised wars, his lack of intellectual ability to recognize changing foreign relations, conditions and his failure to proactively seek out improved relationships with foreign countries, this President had caused America to lose significant credibility in the world.

Colonel Turner told Zachary that they were tracking several targets of interest, but the targets were covering their tracks very well. The bad guys were learning and adapting. Zachary thought back again to his college classes in microbiology, where he learned how a virus adapted and mutated. The virus and the terrorist were ever changing to adapt to conditions in their environment, because both wanted to survive and both were proving adept at achieving this. With adaptation, it was becoming more difficult to connect the dots, and this made each country's leadership nervous.

Zachary told his old friend, "We must work harder. Time is running short. I have this gut feeling that something is afoot. I sense time is short." Colonel Turner told his friend, "I know not having a target to kill, no target to take down, no target to track frustrates you and it frustrates me too." He continued, "It is time to turn up the heat the known targets." The old friends agreed and stated they would move forward with other aggressive tactics to see if this would generate any useful outcomes

Mashir and his friends left the coffee shop and headed downtown. None of them had to work, so they planned to hang out at the local shops and spend time at the park. Mashir told his friends, "I have to go to the mosque today for midday prayers. I will call you guys and catch up with you later this evening." As Mashir entered the mosque, he, along with all other persons entering and leaving had his photograph taken by Army Special Forces surveillance unit. This had been going on for the past several weeks.

After 9-11, new laws allowed the military to exercise its protective powers without worrying about some jurisdictional problem with the local police or some young civil rights attorney or any attorney in general trying to make a name and money for himself by professing to protect the rights of the innocent. 9-11 taught the military that American safeguards created to protect the American masses could not fully achieve safety due to the inability of the various homeland security forces to communicate effectively. Zachary Wilson saw that the most intelligent being on Earth, mankind, could create, could destroy, could extend life, but had never fully figured out the secret of just communicating.

Zachary thought it was sad that the failure to communicate or understand what someone was trying to present had led to many unnecessary deaths and human suffering over the course of mankind's rule of the blue and green marble called Earth.

The photographs from the mosque taken by the high-resolution cameras were quickly fed to the supercomputer located in Quantico, Virginia. The new algorithms developed by IBM from money set aside by Congress after 9-11 worked well, almost too well. The technician running the analysis today thought to himself that the U.S. had to have paid the defense contractor a pretty price for this software. But this was the case for anything labeled a "Homeland Security" priority. Money was being spent on security measures at a rate unheard of in history. Many "no-name companies" had become overnight successes as a result of signing lucrative non-compete contracts with the government. Again, the President's cowboy attitude allowed this to happen even though it was known that many of the firms benefiting from this bounty were from his home State.

In a few moments, the computer recognition software turned up some interesting hits on one young fellow who entered the mosque today. Mashir did not know he had been photographed and proceeded to the back of the mosque to join his friends. Not only was the software able to refine the picture to a high-resolution format, but it allowed the technician to view a person's attributes as if only inches separated the two. The computer recognized and identified the individuals, assuming they had been previously tagged as a person of interest, it also gave demographic, financial, medical, travel, education, legal, and other information on the target. The report also referenced visits to an address of one Abdul al-Kariim.

The report on Mashir showed he had traveled to Jordan several times during the past year. The technician mentally noted that although it was not a crime for someone to travel to a country multiple times in twelve months, it was interesting that a person would travel to a country where he was not born and could afford international travel on such meager earnings. Again, the new software developed by IBM worked like a charm. The technician noted other findings and flagged this person as a target of interest. Once this designation was entered into the computer, Mashir would now be watched not only by the military, but also by a team drawn from multiple agencies all attempting to determine if this

guy intended any mal-intent against the United States.

Unknown to the team, Mashir would exit the mosque

tonight, not on the street corner where he had entered, but through

a tiny opening in the far western corner of the building's basement.

The true believers of Allah would seal the hole and Mashir would

disappear like the air from a dying man's lungs. Never seen, but

the effect of both Mashir's disappearance and the air leaving the

lungs for the last time would have the same effect – death.

The news did not settle well with Zachary. How could they

lose this guy Mashir? Did he leave the mosque in disguise or

through some other means? The security tapes had been reviewed

several times. Over two hundred persons came and left during the

time Mashir had entered the building. Several moving vans and

cars also had left the back of the facility. Mashir could have been

in either one of those. License tags had been obtained from the

videotapes and the whereabouts of each vehicle and its owner

would be run down and analyzed.

This search would be in vain, though, Mashir had long left

the city through the one place an American would never expect a true Muslim to go – the sewer. Mashir, however, was a true believer and knew this trek was the first leg of his journey to the holy land of all Martyrs. He believed in and would lay down his life for the cause.

Zachary was beleaguered. Mashir was gone, the other leads were not turning up information as fast as possible, and his hands were tied as a result of the country's laws. A virus of rebellion had entered the body politic, and had learned to turn on and off its identifying proteins when needed. Zachary told the junior lieutenant, "We can now order phone taps on any person of interest without going through the courts, we have been given wide access to security information and yet, we lose a damn guy who went into a mosque." John, the lieutenant, responded, "Yes sir, this is truly upsetting. The President really doesn't have to fear any election fallout since he is not seeking another term. We've got to do better especially given the fact we have extraordinary freedom to engage the enemy on any and all levels." But wiretaps and reviews of billions of bits of email data just did not work fast enough in this new era of non-traditional warfare. Zachary knew something had to be done. He needed warm bodies to interrogate and he knew he had to obtain permission to begin bringing in folks or did he? He also knew, given the current state of affairs in the country, that the interrogations would need to be done offshore. Zachary then called Colonel McIntosh and told him, "Sir, on my authority, I am initiating Free Fall." Colonel McIntosh realizing Zachary had taken this step knew Zachary must be feeling very uneasy and frightened by what he either knew or did not know. It was the latter point that gave the old Colonel pause. If Zachary was escalating things to this level, something must have occurred. The Colonel asked, "Son what's going on? What happened since we last spoke?" The Colonel continued, "My review of the Intel reports did not show any unusual activity from the targets being tracked. I would like to remind you, Son that you will be held accountable and you alone if the establishment finds out about Operation Free Fall." Zachary told his old friend, "Yes Sir, I understand the rules of engagement and the risk I am assuming." Zachary told the Colonel, "my team was tracking a high value target and we just lost him. He disappeared into thin air. We have photographs of him going into a Los Angles mosque and never exiting the facility. This same guy has traveled to Jordan on several occasions. I would also add, he works minimum wage jobs. So how in the hell can he afford such travel?" Zachary further informed the Colonel, "This Mashir fellow always took lengthy routes when he returned to the States, almost as if he was taking preplanned stops to determine if he were being trailed." Zachary continued, "These were some of the same tactics used by earlier successful attackers against American interests." Colonel McIntosh asked Zachary, "Have the teams tracking the power company executive turned up anything?" Zachary's voice again showed his displeasure with the results to date. The Colonel reminded the young warrior the new tactics and rules of engagement used by the foes in this new war were not consistent with the ways of old. The Colonel told Zachary, "Be careful, but turn up the heat on the suspects where necessary to gain the results needed. "You are correct, sir. We'll keep pressing on", Zachary concluded. Zachary pressed the "end" button on his satellite phone and slammed it to the desk. Zachary then picked up his satellite phone and told the person on the other end to initiate Operation Free Fall.

America, America, where art thou, America of old? Zack wondered. Here he was working as hard as he could to do things that could possibly save the lives of thousands of Americans. Now he had to worry about some civil liberties lawyer dragging his name through the mud because he decided to interrogate some bad guys who may or may not have anything to do with potential plots against America. He thought lawyers really did not care for the person they were defending: they cared more about generating billable hours. The case that would be built if Operation Free Fall was discovered would assure some lawyer and his associates many billable hours.

Zachary would work hard to make sure he covered his trail as well as he had when he and his team worked in the jungle. He knew he needed someone whom he could trust to run the offshore base and someone who was off the radarscope of the establishment. He would need a team of no more than ten to operate the offshore interrogation unit. The funding for this operation would be coordinated so it would not be tracked. The criminal element never figured out how the government was able to uncover schemes such as money laundering. But if the criminal ever took the time to think deeply, he would see that the government used some of the same strategies and tactics used by the criminal element used itself to hide and move money.

So Zachary had no problem getting the money he needed to run Operation Free Fall. Now only one thing remained, who could he trust to be in charge of the Unit? Zachary activated his satellite phone and called his friend Richard. Now, both friends were officially back in the game.

But, on the other side of the globe, another individual at this exact moment was keying a unique code into his Motorola satellite phone. It had begun. Youssef knew Akeem had completed his task, and the timing was right to initiate all phases of the plan.

Chapter 10 – O, Israel

Peace was inevitable. The hardliners from Israel knew what this meant. No conflict with the Arabs meant they would no longer be the center of the West's attention. The lack of attention meant critical influxes of Western cash would be channeled elsewhere. For years, Israel had been able to manipulate the West into believing it was the center of the universe. Israel's position was simple; no Israel, no place flowing with milk and honey, meant no man or woman or child from any Judeo-Christian place on the face of the Earth would ascend to the greater plane of living eternally in the presence of God the Father Almighty.

The Palestinian and Arab people had learned to replace the armed struggle with peace. They had studied the lives and legend of Dr. Martin Luther King and Mahatma Gandhi. The new Arab tactic of turning the other cheek, instead of raising the fist in anger, had relegated Israel's reason for attack to a negative international headline. Now it was Israel under attack, under direction from the West to cease all aggressive military activities against the "peaceful" Palestinian people. The American President told the Israeli Prime Minister, "If non-defensive military operations do not cease immediately, all military and other related appropriations will be drastically reduced!"

Not only did the President have the will to carry this out, he also had the backing of Congress, since the demographics of the United States had changed significantly over the past thirty years. No longer a bastion of the White Anglo-Saxon Protestant, America was now a browner society. Years of immigration from Africa, the Middle East, South America, and Central America had shifted the demographics and subsequently the country's politics. The United States was built on the backs of enslaved Africans who were brought to this country not by their free will. -Today's paid servants although not forced to come to this country, the immigrants from South America and Mexico are offered menial jobs and are housed for the most part in sub-par housing. The changing American demographics had also shifted the historical support of the country for Israel. The formation of alliances between the sons and daughters of former slaves with the sons and daughters of the new era's paid slaves – Mexican and South American immigrants, resulted in Israel's not being seen in the same light as before. Yes, the Jews' influence in the American

Congress had waned. The Israeli leader knew his country's tactic of inciting the Arab was now ineffective. A new strategy would be needed, if his country were to survive.

The meeting was planned for eight o'clock in the morning. The Israeli Prime Minister was first to arrive, a chubby gray-haired gentleman. He looked like the great toy-carrying St. Nicholas rather than the leader of the smallest, most armed country in the world. This gentleman had fought for his country and had killed many Arabs. Having been raised to believe anyone with browner skin than his was dangerous, the era of non-violence made him and his fellow countrymen extremely uneasy.

The Israeli leader did not want this meeting. He wanted war. With war, he could easily identify the problem, plan for its eradication, and carry out the necessary attack. He knew the attack could be evaluated based on the number killed and the calm or lack thereof that followed. Those were the outcomes that drove the investment in his country. War, not peace, produced the need for the American defense industry to invest billions in congressional lobbying. For their investment, Congress supported

Israel and Israel purchased billions of dollars in defense equipment.

Today the Israeli leader would attempt to evaluate his new nemesis, the Palestinian President. This man who would soon sit across the table from him had figured it out. Peace, not war, was the cancer Israel feared. Peace although publicly called for by all was only a cover to lead the West into thinking this was indeed the desire of his people. The Israelis did not want peace; they wanted and needed war. Today, he and his negotiators would probe the Palestinian leader to determine his weaknesses, and these exposed weaknesses would be exploited. The Israelis knew that exploitation of a political rival's weakness was one way to fan the flames of war. Yes, they would figure out how to rekindle the way of their ancestors. War was good; war brought in billions from the West; and war was a measurable objective with outcomes that could be reported to its people. Israel would not go peacefully into the bowels of history.

The young Palestinian leader, educated in the West, fully understood the goal and tenor of today's meeting. He could tell that the delegation from Israel was testing him to see what made him work. He also knew by his training that these initial probes would be followed by more intense attempts to undermine his leadership and the fragile peace he and his supporters had recently forged. The Israeli Prime Minister was interested in how he planned to work with his country to disband the hundreds of settlements now pock-marking the landscape of Jericho and the land formerly owned by the Palestinians.

Prior to that fateful day in 1948 after the British mandate over Palestine expired, the Jews declared the illegal free state of Israel. The young leader knew this would be the first of many ploys by his country's enemy. He would handle each as delicately as he had handled each of his three young children after their birth. Nothing would deter him from rubbing peace in the face of the aggressors. Like their Western protector, the United States, Israel only knew war and conquering. Peace to Israel meant death, and it was Israel's death the young leader was intent on bringing. It was interesting, and to some extent funny, the young leader thought, death by the butter knife, not by the sword. Yes, this would be a most enjoyable sparring for him – great intellectual and emotional sport!

With the planned action in the United States and the impact of lowered funding by Western interests in Israel, he knew the Israelis would be in trouble. No longer able to support its military or economy, the country built on lies and deceit would spiral into the sewer of destruction without one bomb or one Palestinian death. However, he also knew Israel was strong, witty, and had more than one deck of cards to play.

What he feared most was his followers' inability to have patience as the negative, aggressive responses from Israel flowed. He also knew one play could be an attack on himself or his family creating the inability for him to lead his countrymen to their promised land. He hoped his Western-trained security detail was up to the challenge. In case they were not, the Uzi he carried underneath his oversized jacket and the body armor tailor-made for him would ensure he would not go easily - unless the end came from a headshot.

His family was another matter. His family never traveled in the convoys but took less noticeable transportation to move about. It was nothing for his wife and children to be saddled on donkeys or camels with only two bodyguards. These men guarding his family were his most trusted associates. He had

forged friendships with them since childhood. In many instances

he had put his life on the line to save the lives of their families --

and for this, they had pledged their lives to protect his family.

At lunchtime each delegation went to their respective hotels

for rest and food. The meeting would reconvene in three hours.

The young Palestinian leader, Ahmed Al-Homs was American

educated and understood the customs of the capitalist. He also

knew the economic importance of America's blind support of the

Jew. He would need all of his American training as he knew the

discussions would increase in intensity. The young leader

convened his meeting with his close associates. Al-Homs started

the meeting by stating, "My brothers, we must remain patient and

we must make certain our people remain patient. We will obtain

our rights for a free Palestinian state not by the sword by the olive

branch of peace. Please my brothers, our future and the future of

our people living in a free state of Palestine rest on our shoulders."

All in the room listened intently to their Al-Homs. One of the

delegation members asked, "What do we do should Israel begin the

secret death squads against our people?" Al-Homs replied, "Many of our people have died to gain peace for our people. Many more my die before we achieve this peace we all seek." They all agreed, patience was indeed a virtue and they knew Israel was running short of it. With increasing pressure from Western countries to accept the Palestinian olive branch of peace, the Israeli leadership knew something had to be done quickly rather than later. For years protecting Israel had been the West's excuse to invade the Middle East in the name of democracy. However, many had come to see the invasions as a ploy to drain the Middle-Eastern countries of their oil.

Now that China, India, and other developing nations' economies were demanding almost as much oil as the U.S., alliances and support were shifting like the sand blown on a hot Arabian wind. America no longer needed Israel to serve as its anchorage in the Middle East. As everyone in the U.S. establishment had known for years, this anchorage only served as an American watch tower over the region's vast oil reserves. Yet, Israel still needed America. Israel no longer worried about its struggle with God. It now had to worry about its existence in a world where its strength could be taken away by the mere thought of peace. Yes, Israel spoke of peace, but it was not peace the leaders of this country wanted. They wanted war and the billions of dollars received from the West.

The groups met once again after their lunch break. The Israeli Prime Minister Abidya asked, "Mr. Al-Homs what can do to show my people that you want peace with Israel. How can the Israeli people trust those who had slaughtered so many Jews? How can my people trust a modern-day Hitler? Whether by gas or by bomb, death was death, and many Israelis had their lives shortened as a result of misguided Palestinian terrorists."

Mr. Al-Homs was prepared. He wanted to remind the Jew, the bigot, the man who called himself a man of God, this man whose name means "father of knowledge", that it was Israel who killed and stole land. He wanted to remind him of Israel's unofficial take-over of Jerusalem and naming it as its capital city. But the young leader held his harsh words. He knew instinctively that the Israeli leader's tirade was the last gasp of a desperate man. Like a person drowning in the ocean's waves, the Israeli leader was attempting to cling to life, and these were the actions of a dying man, speaking for a dying country. With the clouds of peace on the horizon, Israel was in big trouble unless changes could be made quickly. Mr. Al-Homs, responded to the outburst in a slow deliberate manner, "President Abidya, many Israelis have died. Many of my people have died. Whether we believe you were fighting for the right to protect your people or whether we the Palestinians were fighting to reclaim the land and the freedoms we once had, and most importantly whether we all were fighting to reclaim the love for our brothers as you know we all come from the same origins, it is time to stop fighting. On behalf of the Palestinian people, I offer you our olive branch of peace."

The young leader of the soon-to-be Palestinian state knew he had won this battle. His instincts also told him he had just started a war. Not a war between nations but a war between individual men. For this he would have to be on guard for all eternity to safeguard his family. His life could be given for the sake of his people, but he would not allow his wife or children to come into harm's way. If he were to meet an untimely unexplained death, this would be a message to the rest of the world that Israel was not the land of milk and honey, but was a place of blood, sweat, tears and death. His death would also tell the world that Israel did not want peace. This would cause the world to move its support away from Israel and would bring on death to this country that was built on the blood of Al-Homs ancestors. The Young Leader had won the initial battle for his countrymen and only hoped he would live to see his children live free in a country of their own. Al-Homs was taking the Israeli land not by the force of the hand, but by the force of the brain, thanks to his Western education. His knowledge of history told him he had beaten the old warrior.

President Abidya knew the Israeli people would not accept this loss. The failure of the Israeli leader to generate anger in Al-Homs would expedite the decline of the Israeli State. The old battle-hardened Israeli leader had attempted all of the tactics he knew to throw off the young Palestinian leader. Frustrated, he knew a change was on the horizon for his country, a new day not filled with milk and honey. Instead, it would be an agonizing death at the hands of the people who had wanted to see them eradicated for centuries. This fear, this failure, and this humiliation at the hands of such a young adversary led to his anger.

As the anger within the old Israeli leader became more apparent, the young leader himself became afraid. The look on the old warrior's face did not show the look of a beaten foe; instead his was the face of death. Death he knew would now come for many in his country, as he knew the Israelis would deploy resources at their disposal to destabilize the Palestinian leadership. The young leader knew what would come next. Israel would not stand idly by and watch the gains made over centuries of struggle end up in the abyss of extinction. Instead, the Israeli's last gasp would be like that of a dying hurricane.

As a hurricane moves ashore, the winds on the front side of the storm do not cause the worst damage. The winds on the back end of the storm do the most damage. Those winds coming at the end of the storm's life bring the full brunt of the storm to the inhabitants of seaside towns. The goal of the Israeli leader was to bring the winds of similar destruction to the Arabs who would now celebrate the death of his country. But before his country died, many Arabs would feel the evil winds that were now forming.

Al-Homs, the Palestinian leader knew he would have to use all of his Western education and negotiating skills to make certain his countrymen and women continued to practice a response of non-aggression. He also knew he would need to bring to bear his new alliances with Russia and China. If his people began fighting back, all of the support they had gained incrementally from the West would erode. Actually, he knew that some in the West wanted an armed response to any Israeli aggression. The young leader knew China's and Russia's emergence as economic and now reemerged military powers would not only stem the response of the Israelis, but it would also head off any direct involvement from the United States. The United States did not want to risk a direct military confrontation with either Russia or China. Yet, he knew too close an alliance with either Russia or China would lead to Palestine's becoming a puppet state of a different set of infidels.

The young leader would never see the day he constantly dreamed of. His fate was sealed with the outcome of the meeting. Unknown too many, the Israelis had run a highly successful counter-espionage program in the United States. Having stolen hundreds of secrets, these now had been developed to meet the need of the Israeli military and secret police. For many years, the United States had developed systems aimed at taking out seemingly untouchable targets. These assets had never been used, as the United States did not want to set the precedent of pre-emptive strikes against foreign leaders. Israel did not have this moderate philosophy. Like an animal, Israel would attack if provoked, would strike if it thought another was a threat. The Old Warrior leader had determined the young leader of the yet-to-be defined Palestinian State met both conditions.

Deep beneath the Temple Mount, Israel had a series of top-secret research facilities. The research facilities purposely were placed below the Temple Mount, as the Israelis felt this would be the last place any country would attack, for fear of a joint response from Arab and Christian societies. These facilities enlisted the services of many top Israeli scientists in addition to some hired hands from other countries. The scientists took the secrets stolen from the West, made modifications, and developed these for their own use. These systems would mean instant death to anyone who threatened Israel's existence. The field of microscopic robotics had intensified and expanded tremendously with the advent of smaller electronic components. Using the process of reverse engineering, Israeli scientists had improved many inventions created by the United States and other Western nations' scientists.

One such project was Locust. The Israeli scientists had chosen this name because of the plagues caused by this insect over the centuries. Project Locust, like the actual insect, was meant to cause death. Unlike the actual insect that could be seen as it swarmed from field to field, this locust would not be seen. It would strike silently and quickly. The Locust, as the Project Team fondly called it, was a small microscopic-sized killing machine. Designed to deliver a highly toxic nerve agent through a hypodermic injection system, it was truly an amazing design.

The size of a fruit fly, the system containing the injection system was basically a specially designed hypodermic needle fired when specialized pistons produced enough air pressure to push the needle towards its intended target. The scientists had been successful in developing microscopic air pumps that would force air pressure through a series of capillaries. As the air flowed through the capillaries, narrower near the needle's point, the air pressure would increase. This increase in pressure would propel the needle to the target at a high rate of speed. The hypodermic needle was loaded with a weapon zed nerve agent that would kill the target in seconds. After testing it on large animals like elephants and buffalo, the scientists knew Locust would bring a quick death to its quarry. Small wings propelled the Locust through the air. The casual observer would think the Locust was a fruit fly, nothing to bother about. The typical day's activities were more important than trying to swat something so small and insignificant.

The coded message to the Israeli Secret Police was simple, "The Young will turn old and die." Unknown to him and his handlers, during the meeting, the Young Palestinian leader had been tagged with a special dye. This dye contained materials that could be tracked by special sensors on the Locust. Thus, knowing the location of Al-Homs would be simple. The release of the Locust was even simpler. The Locust would be released from a car driven by the Palestinian Leader's residence one week after his return from the conference with Israel. Locust sensors would quickly pick up on the trail of the dye and quickly locate its quarry.

On the prescribed morning, Al-Homs, the Palestinian leader was in his private residence playing with his son. Al-Homs asked his young son, Tamer, "What he wanted to be when he grew up?" His young son replied, "An airline pilot daddy." The young boy had grown use to the many planes that flew over the countryside and always ran with his arms spread wide when he saw one overhead. In many Middle Eastern countries, people leave their windows open to take advantage of the beautiful breezy mornings. Unfortunately, the wind entering the Al-Homs residence carried the dye's aroma to the Locust. So, the Locust quickly flew into the residence. Its onboard cameras sent pictures back via satellite to operators in Jerusalem. It was almost like watching the play-by-play of a soccer game. The picture of young leader in the Locust's camera grew larger as the Locust closed in on its quarry.

Just like that, the Young Leader was down, and the last image shown was Tamer, his young son running from the room. The Locust, after delivering its package, was pre-set to end its life, just like a real fruit fly dies after mating. The Locust had met its mate, and its mate had been born again. Only the birth was death, and the death was birth into the after-life. Being tiny the Locust would be swept up the next morning as the residence of Al-Homs was cleaned to prepare for his State funeral. The toxin used was metabolized quickly by the body and would not be discovered by any test run by Russian or Chinese scientists. Yes, Israel would bring death; like the winds of a dying hurricane, to many.

The death of the Young Leader hit the news wires across the world. The Young Leader of the planned new Palestinian state was dead, seemingly from a heart attack. For the next several weeks, Russian and Chinese scientists would analyze tissue and blood samples in an attempt to determine if indeed he met his maker from natural causes. Al-Homs was known to be in excellent health with open access to the best physicians trained at Western medical facilities. His medical records were analyzed to determine whether he had maintained a preventive maintenance routine, including maintaining good cholesterol levels. The Chinese and Russian scientists met dead ends at every turn. Condolences flowed in from foreign leaders from across the globe. The state funeral was set to occur two weeks after his death. Time was needed to plan for the arrival and security needs of many foreign dignitaries.

The death of the young leader did not mean anything personal to Zachary Carson Wilson. However, Zachary knew this would drain intelligence assets from his task of tracking and finding Scarlet Badge's cells and uncovering any planned activities. Zachary instinctively knew that Israel probably had robbed the young leader of his final days on Earth. The Young Leader had exhibited too much independent thought for him to be tolerated by the mainstream. He elicited and provoked public thoughts of a homeland separate from Israel with Jerusalem as its capital city.

Israel would not stand for this. The Young Leader's ability to establish and craft a message for the world to understand posed a major risk to Israel's existence. Zachary knew the way of the world: threats had to be eradicated. This at least was the rule outside of America's borders. In America, however, perpetrators were innocent until proven guilty, and that meant someone had to die or be harmed first. A crime had to be committed before anything was done. In order to determine whether a true threat existed against America, Zachary needed resources. He knew his resources now would be limited as America attempted to

determine what had caused the Al-Homs's untimely death.

Chapter 11 – Mother's Day

For Abdul, the day was atypical. He had lost his mother to an Israeli bomb that had gone astray. Now the only female who mattered to him was his wife. He had planned this day for many weeks. He wanted this day to be special for his young wife. She had done without so much as he struggled to provide bare necessities for his young family. Yet, Malik, his son, the love of his life, did not know the things he lacked, for Abdul had taught him not to measure success by the acquisition of materialistic things, but only by those deeds that helped others.

Abdul had awakened early to prepare his wife her favorite breakfast, for today was special. The day would include a walk with Malik in tow, to the park after breakfast in bed. The city in the morning was a beautiful place. With their apartment so close to downtown, it was an easy walk to the inner city park. Flowers were in full bloom, and Abdul had bought a lovely bouquet late last night and hidden them in a glass vase before going to bed. Christina awakened right on time - 8:00 a.m.; and came downstairs. Even without preparing herself for the day, in Abdul's eyes she was as beautiful as the morning star and the evening dew.

She was not only beautiful in appearance, but her spirit of caring made her even more endearing. Abdul greeted his wife with a hug and kiss while whispering in her ear, "You are my desert flower and I love you." Their togetherness was broken by the sound of the young Malik running out of his room yelling, "What's for breakfast? I want pancakes. Mommy can I have some grapes? Do we have any grape juice?" Both parents looked at each other knowingly understanding the look in each other's eyes – What have we created?

After breakfast the family struck out for the park. Christina holding her husband's hand told him, "I love the peacefulness of this place. I wish it was this peaceful at the clinic." As they walked, the rays of the rising eastern sun shined on them as if they were on a stage under the lights. Abdul, told his son, "Be careful and watch for other people walking." Malik was skipping and running ahead of his parents. As they passed the mosque, Abdul could make out several familiar figures standing outside. Odd they would be there at this time of the day, he thought to himself. Christina and Malik, "Please wait here. I'm going to speak to my friends. I will not be long." As he approached the group, they recognized their friend and welcomed him to their morning discussions. "Good morning Brother Abdul." Abbas, who had the body build of an old dessert lion, asked Abdul, "Brother what are you doing today." Abdul told the group, "I am going to the park to spend time with my wife and child. I made my wife breakfast in bed this morning." The group of men had all come to America around the same time from their home countries. All had come to America seeking opportunities to improve their lives.

Many had been pushed by their parents to leave their homeland for fear they would be lost in the armed struggle against the infidels in Israel. Each had come to America and had staked their future on an ability to find a niche where their skills would meet the need of some capitalist. Akil told Abdul, "Please come by the mosque tonight if you have time. We have so much to tell you about the blessing of Allah." But this group had been changed unbeknownst to Abdul. They had been hardened as they watched the continued destruction of their homeland by Israel with help from the America they had come to seeking opportunity.

They were the free radicals, floating in the American cytoplasmic soup. As with Mad Cow Disease, thought to be caused by free radical proteins from infected cow's meat, Abdul's friends had become the free radicals of the Islamic religion living in America. Given the right environment, free radicals can cause severe havoc within an organism's body. Abdul pointed out his waiting family across the street and told his friends he would see them later in the day.

Unknown to Abdul, this would be the last time he would ever see these men again. As with an earthquake fault line, the pressure of U.S. interventions throughout the world had built up potential energy along several fault lines now on the verge of erupting with catastrophic results. As his friends watched him return to his family, they all agreed it was unfortunate Abdul would not be able to join them in Paradise. Although he had remained true to his religion, he was married to a Westerner – an American at that - making him too much of a security risk. Just as well, someone had to be left behind. After the action they planned, maybe more of their countrymen would be inspired to become true believers – that was their hope.

Abdul, Malik, and Christina continued their walk to the park. It was a lovely sunny morning. Malik ran ahead and Abdul allowed himself to wonder what type of life his young son would have. He and Christina would do all they could do to assure his life was better than theirs. Not only would they instill in him the tenets of their religious beliefs, but they would also teach their son the importance of a strong work ethic. One thing they both had come to know and strongly believe was that true self-preservation did not come from working for others for a long period of time. The people in this country who truly controlled their destiny only worked for others for a short period of time. Those who projected a true entrepreneurial spirit and acted on their own ideas were rewarded with great wealth.

Before they entered the park Abdul asked his wife, "Do you want to stop by Starbucks for coffee." She responded, "Yes, that would be great and we can get our little firebug a blue berry muffin." The park brimmed with life as the city's inhabitants began another day trying to fulfill their primitive urges to re-link to nature, a hard feat in this city, this jungle of steel and concrete. Nature indeed had adapted to this new jungle as numerous stories abounded of wildlife moving into this newly created forest. It was not unusual for bears, mountain lions, and other creatures to be spotted in the city. Many pets had gone astray; leaving the owner to believe their pet would come home. Unknown to the owner, their poor pet had become dinner for a hungry cougar.

Malik ran over to the swing. He loved for his father to push him high. "Daddy", he yelled, "Push me as high as you can." The momentary feeling of weightlessness at the top of the arc allowed him to pretend he was an astronaut. Abdul pushed his son while Christina browsed among the flowers in the garden. The insects that depended on this oasis in the city were sapping up their daily supply of nectar. This would be used to fuel their insect economy. Nectar, like oil, was the life blood of any beehive. Bees, like humans, had a complex society, with workers, soldiers, leaders, and free loaders, the drones. So too does human society. Man truly is more like the simple creatures on the planet than he is the supposed master of his environment. He spends every waking hour on how to make it through the day without becoming the victim of someone else's desire to consume another. For this reason, man like bees, has developed defense systems so that those with ill will think twice before launching an attack. Man, like a bee, stings too!

Malik called, "Father, push me higher into the air!" Malik asked, "Where will we eat lunch today?" His growing son was developing a very healthy appetite. Abdul and Christina always provided their young son with the best. Malik was given the things he needed, and was never made to feel that more was better or necessary. Abdul wanted to make certain his son would grow to be respectful of the laws and customs of this great country and would treat his fellow American with respect and care. Only through these values would one be able to help the leaders of the country maintain control over the masses. Abdul did not want Malik to become an ant, blindly following the chemical scent of his leaders, or on the other hand, a rebel who would spend his life in prison. He wanted his son to have the intelligence and the confidence in his own abilities to think without being told what to think, a free man. This was becoming less of an option as the government became more engaged in providing information to misinform the masses in order to maintain control.

Abdul and Christina spent many waking hours discussing the future they wanted for their child. They sometimes wondered if they would ever see the day where their young child could truly compete fairly for his position in the great circle of life. With America's economy becoming more of a service-based industry and many high-tech jobs being transferred offshore, the American pie was becoming smaller. America's training arm of its industrial complex, the colleges and universities, were still producing students, but they were trained in areas where the jobs were being filled by persons in China, India, and other newly developing industrialized countries. A direct result of globalization, cheaper wages went to employees in other countries who possessed the same educational level and, in many instances, a greater drive to produce a quality product than their American counterparts.

In America, youth had become complacent. Young Americans had grown up on MTV, HBO, Game Cube, and Play Station instead of reading, writing, and arithmetic. Thus it was a shock to many after four years of college to find themselves right back in the bedroom of their parents' house. Often, college graduates could not find a job that met their misguided belief that the world was theirs. The world was no longer the playground for Americans. Globalization was increasing the opportunities for many other youth from afar to compete for American dollars.

Youth in China and India were taking advantage of opportunity, in nations where $20,000 a year would place a person on the top of the economic pedestal. Thus, American companies moved jobs offshore, where they still received the highest quality result at less than half the cost. The American pie was no longer the rich Apple Pie baked in America from 1946 – 2000.

Malik was enjoying his day at the park. He ran from the monkey bars back to the swings. In the distance, rising above the tree line, he could see the tall buildings of the city. "Mommy, how do people build such tall buildings", he yelled. Christina responded, "Honey, people called engineers and architects design the buildings and construction men and women use those designs to build the final structure. Maybe one day you will be an engineer or architect."

Malik told his mother, "I want to be a professional baseball player, not a designer of buildings." Abdul listened intently as he too had lived this dream. He would support his young son in any way possible. One thing for sure, his son would master his schoolwork, as Abdul knew the dream of becoming a professional baseball player could be short-circuited at any point. Finally, it was lunchtime.

Chapter 12: Thirteen miles

Mohammed was not a superstitious man. Being a true believer did not afford him the opportunity to believe in anything else but his role in life to serve Allah. Mohammed was happy with the batteries' performance. He knew he needed this performance if they were to be successful.   Many years of education in the United States had prepared the young Arab for this day. He had received his doctorate in Electrical and Chemical Engineering from North Carolina State University. He then honed his skills working with several major chemical firms in the United States before being converted to a true believer.

The batteries would be shipped out tonight to the Lebanese seaport of El Mina. There they would be fitted on their hosts, subs made by the American company that makes recreational subs used by tourists to view the wonders of the undersea. These subs were built to carry two people at a maximum depth of thirty feet at a speed of fifteen miles per hour. The two persons were required to wear exterior air tanks, but this would be no problem. The teams who would use these subs would carry extra tanks to insure they had plenty of oxygen to reach their intended destination. Six subs, twelve true believers would deal a major blow against the Great Satan's seaports.

It was truly amazing and yet simplistic how Americans allowed themselves to be deceived by their leaders. Of all of the billions of dollars allocated to Homeland Security after that great day in September of the year 2001, America was no safer. Much of the money had gone to defense contractors and other supporters of the American President who gave part of the money back to his re-election campaign. America's borders were as open as ever: thousands of illegal immigrants still migrated from Central America and Mexico each year, along with a few others whose national origin was many miles away across the vast Atlantic Ocean. Mohammed knew that the teams who would attack America's interior had been in place for several months and had in fact transversed the border from Juarez, Mexico, with the help of a Mexican smuggler, who incidentally did not live long enough to accept his fee.

Mohammed would accompany the batteries to Lebanon in order to oversee their installation into the subs. His knowledge of battery-generated power, especially ways to increase their efficiency and longevity, was needed by the movement. It would take the cargo ship ten days to complete the journey across the ocean to the Port of New Orleans. No ordinary cargo ship, the ship had been modified years before just for this mission. One thing Allah teaches all of his followers is patience and the importance of careful planning. Patience and perseverance were traits the Great Country of Satan; America did not have. America was a land of the rich and the mighty, and they quickly forgot the past in order to benefit from the next business deal planned for the future.

America did have a memory. However, the pain of the memory did not invoke a sense of fear. Thus the country never truly developed the defenses needed to protect its people. If America followed the traits of nature, it would have remembered the attacks from the past and its systems would have picked up quickly on some of the identical activities happening in the present that had begun before September 11, 2001. America did not treat the attack of 9-11 as an attack by a small body. In fact, it responded with might, to wipe out the cause of the attack while forgetting to eliminate the microscopic cells that had caused the growth that generated the 9-11 attack. Had the Americans treated the 9-11 attack as a radiation oncologist treats cancer, then the cells of the cause would have been the focus of the American response to 9-11. Instead, it treated Iraq and Afghanistan as the only staging grounds for the attacks against itself, like a surgeon cutting out a tumor without first determining whether the tumor had spread. America's defenses should have been trained after 9-11 to identify viruses, not organs. Unfortunately, the American President was more interested in organs, and thus set the country's defense mechanism behind many years as it primarily tracked threats from nation-states, not cells.

The ship would launch covert operations through an undersea hatch. Because, the American Coast Guard was severely undermanned, the Guard's Commander had fought hard to obtain more funding for his forces. He could not understand how billions of dollars were being spent to prop up governments in foreign countries when in fact the defenses of this county went without. Anyone inside the establishment knew it was only a matter of time before the next attack would occur. Yes, America would respond, but why could it not act first to prevent the attack? America, unfortunately, had become a country built on retrospective action instead of prospective action.

Scarlet Badge knew that if a ship was going to be inspected, that would occur once the ship was within twelve of the American coastline. The subs would need to be launched at the thirteenth mile. The trip to Lebanon was uneventful, and Mohammed allowed himself to think of the wonders that lay ahead. A few would affect the lives of the many. It was not the thought of killing or scaring innocent people that drove people like him. His people, the followers of the one true God --Allah -- only wanted peace, to be left to govern as the Koran implied. No one had invited the Anglos to this side of the world; they had invited themselves. For many centuries, his forefathers dreamed of the day when they could fight back with more than stones and arrows. Satan, America, answered their prayers by opening its borders to their children, to educate them in hopes they too would be converted to their kind. Many had fallen for the tricks of greed and the new creed that a healthy financial portfolio was the only way to live out one's existence on earth. Yes, many of his kind had taken-up the creed of the non-believers, the Infidels.

The fresh smell of seawater announced their arrival in El Mina. He and his driver followed the narrow street to the dock where Jafa met them. Jafa was happy to see his older cousin. From his youth on, Jafa had always looked to Mohammed for guidance. Both had grown up in Syria in a large family. Their parents attempted to shield them from the brutality of the fight against Israel and the United States. Even so, many of their friends joined the movement at an early age and now had gone on to join Allah and the other martyrs. Mohammed's father sought more for his young son and when Mohammed was of age, he sent him to live with his brother in England. Eventually Mohammed's penchant for chemistry and mathematics led him to seek opportunity abroad. A chance encounter with an engineering recruiter led him to enroll in the North Carolina State University's electrical and mechanical engineering program. Despite the distance, Mohammed stayed in contact with his younger cousin and sent money when he could.

The next morning Mohammed installed the batteries on the subs and ran the final checks. Each battery package met the required specifications and insured that at least this part of the plan was ready to go. In order to protect those along the line, Mohammed would never see or meet the individuals who would rely on his knowledge of how to corral electricity in small square wafers, the sub's batteries. He knew that like himself, they had a role to play; and they would be dependent on the ability of the sub to take them to their final destination if necessary -- and to their meeting with Allah.

The ship pulled out from port at 7:30 p.m. in order to take advantage of the ebbing tide. Each member of the team settled in for the long voyage. They knew now was the time to prepare themselves mentally for the strenuous tasks that lay ahead.

Chapter 13 - Remission

Youssef and his family had settled into their surroundings very well. Given his status in the network, Youssef received all of the luxuries necessary to someone of his stature. His hosts were grateful to be in his service and were sure it would pay off for them in the long run. The message requesting the key information came as expected. The sun rose on the horizon, yellow and orange, vibrant strands of photoelectrons, diffused by the haze of pollution from the world's lungs belching their poison of Capitalism. Youssef knew this would soon be the color seen by thousands of Americans. But this color would be hot, and if you found yourself too close to the source, like the sun, it would burn you.

Youssef keyed the code into the satellite phone and hung up. The nice thing about the technocrat; those geeks who made the electronic toys of the rich, was that they constantly made gadgets that made his work easier. The diagrams needed by his associates were stored on secure flash memory cards on the shelf of a local grocery store located in San Francisco, California. The memory cards had been marked, "Damaged return to vendor." To the casual observer, it would not seem obvious that these contained some of the secrets to the next plot after 9-11. The casual observer would buy his Coke and see the four cards lying on the shelf and think the poor storeowner had received damaged goods from Kodak.

After sending the information to the "home of the free," Youssef went into the garden where his young daughter was chasing a butterfly through the beautiful flowers. "Be careful and watch the ropes", he called out to his young daughter. She replied back in her soft voice, "I will Papa." As he watched, he dreamed of her growing up to adulthood in a world where the things he had planned would no longer be needed. In this world people would be treated as equal, not lesser vessels to be broken at will by those who thought their beliefs or color of their skin gave them the right to attack and conquer.

As he followed his daughter dashing in and out of the beautiful flowers, why, Youssef wondered, did mankind treat each other with such disrespect? Wars caused the death of many of God's creations. Although he knew questioning his God was against his religion, he wondered why Allah placed his people in such a position to be as mistreated as they had been throughout history.

Yes, his ancestors had also killed and maimed many in Spain, Vienna, Hungary and the Holy Lands for 200 years after 1095, but at this point all Youssef wanted was peace. Peace for his family and peace for his country. Unfortunately, his desire to have peace and many efforts to achieve this through peaceful means had been walked on and over by the Israeli puppets of the United States of America. So Youssef would unleash the fear of death on the Americans to a point where they would need to concentrate on the security of their great country, thus leaving the small Israeli tribe to fend for itself. Once the Israelis were unprotected, he would unleash the greatest attack on one people the world had ever seen. No longer were massive armies and machinery needed to wipe out a race of people. The military of the new millennium was so small and undetectable; it could be in position for an attack well before its enemy knew.

He wished for some other way to express his concerns to the masses. But he knew that this, like his thoughts, were only the dreams of a man searching for Utopia. His daughter Hasayn, like her name, was indeed a beautiful child. She had taken her features from her mother who had caught Youssef's eye one day in the market in England. The two quickly became acquainted, years of happiness followed as his wife supported his drive to become a successful businessman. Latif, his wife, was a gentle woman who provided him the freedom and support to do those things she knew were necessary, not only for the protection of her family, but also for the protection of all Arabs. When Hasayn saw her father standing in the garden, she ran to him as she typically did, knowing he would pick her up and raise her high into the sky. Though young, she knew she was loved and she knew the peace of security. Yes, Youssef was indeed the protector of his family and unknown to his daughter, a destroyer of the peace when he had to be.

The young man standing at the counter in front of the store clerk placed his Coke and other items on the countertop for purchasing. However, today would not be a simple purchase. The arrangement of his clothing, the combination of the things he bought, the look in his eyes all told the store clerk everything he needed to know. Along with the goods he sought to purchase, the man would also receive four flash memory cards marked "Damaged--Return to Vendor." It had begun.

Jason had long given up on his country. Born into a rich family that made its millions on importing cheap goods from China and Mexico, he saw that his family turned a blind eye to the needy. Jason knew this was not his path in life. Numerous times he had seen his family have the opportunity to help those less fortunate, but avoided doing so. Too many times he had sat at the dinner table hearing his mother and father fill the room with excuses for why their way was the right way and those who had less had chosen to be where they were and did not need their help. Jason had tried to persuade his father to use his financial might to help others. Jason specifically remembered one night as the family prepared for their meal, a sense of calm entered the room. Earlier that day, Jason had gotten into trouble at his school for carrying illicit drugs on campus. His father being who he was in the community was able to make a few calls and just like that the event was erased from Jason's record as if someone had spilled Clorox bleach on a clothing stain. However the calm was interrupted as Jason's father asked, "Son what in the hell were you thinking. Your mother and I have worked hard all of our lives so that you can have an easier path in this world. All we want is the ability to insure your future. Why do you disengage from us and do things that just don't make sense?" Jason gave his parents the normal look of – are you finished yet? Jason's quiet response told his father everything that he needed, yet did not want to know. His son was lost, did not care and was rebelling against him. This frustrated his father extremely. Yes, he knew he had missed many opportunities with his son when he was young. His father not joining the young Jason to play in the back yard, opportunities missed for youth sports, never truly learning who his son was and was becoming. His father had left this to Jason's mother as he built his financial empire, the empire he now knew would have no future leader. His father had given up on his son who failed to follow him into Yale University and did not have his drive to excel at business and finance. Instead Jason's choice in life was the Peace Corps after two years at State College.

Jason told his father, "I know you are not happy with me. My path in life will not follow your's. You have built your legacy on the backs of the poor. My legacy will be helping the poor rebuild their lives so that they too can stand straight like you. You continue to build your financial empire and I will build my human empire. An empire that is built of a foundation of compassion for my fellow human, not on the discarded carcasses of dead workers poisoned by the chemical in the materials they use to build the wares that you sell." Jason continued, "Dad you see those at the bottom of the economic totem pole only as pawns in your quest to build an even larger financial empire. Unfortunately, I do not see it that way."

Jason's mom was a sad vessel. Bred to be an aristocratic mate of the rich, she longed only for those things that assured her ability to attend her Thursday tea and go on her weekend shopping trips. When it came to the nurturing of her children, she left this part of life up to the hired help. Jason's relationship with the nanny Zaki allowed him to learn early about other ways of living and the struggles of persons less fortunate than himself. It was this relationship with Zaki that led Jason to believe his legacy would be based on what he did to advance the lives of his fellow human being.

Zaki's family had come to America from Jordan fleeing war and death. Zaki had lost three brothers to the armed conflict with Israel, a fact she kept from every member of Jason's family except him. His nanny had taught him early about the writings of the Koran. In some ways, the Koran was similar to the Bible. In essence it taught the reader to, do well, help others, and above all do no harm. Radicals on both sides continued to use their interpretations of each religion's holy text to move forward their vision of what the world should look like. Whether it was to kill the infidels or bomb the terrorists, radicals on both sides continued to use war and unrest as a means to move their agenda forward.

Zaki taught young Jason that an agenda of war and unrest produced a need for materials and trade. If one were to study history, one would easily see that many of the major economic turnarounds in history occurred during, or soon after, periods of war and unrest. As he grew older, Jason began to apply his teachings from Zaki to the things he saw in the world. He grew amazed how the American masses overlooked the obvious—like blind zombies all moving forward in the game of life, they seemed to be blinded by some mind-controlling substance. Jason knew the mind-controlling substance, Money, was the capitalist's reward for conquering others.

Early on in his young adulthood, though unbeknown to his family, his conversion to Islam was a natural progression to his current state of belief. Unknown to his parents and friends, Jason adopted the Arabic name Seif al Din, which means Sword of the Faith. Jason knew one day he would be called upon to attack his homeland, and it would be his faith that supported his sword.

Jason and his cell were considered the planters. Their job was to deliver the bombs to the power substations that ringed Los Angeles and Las Vegas. The destruction of these substations would cause chaos throughout the Western region of the United States. The power surges caused by the massive shutdown of the key power-conducting systems in the region would automatically result in other systems automatically shutting down their power grids to protect themselves. Medical, financial, domestic, and industrial services would be impacted. It would take weeks for the power company to repair the damage, as the arrogance of their corporate elite never gave them the vision to fathom a terrorist attack on installations such as the power grid's substations;

substations were protected by nothing more than a chained link fence! The Planters would also hit installations of opportunity; including sewage pumping stations, water plants, and cellular towers. With many companies and individuals utilizing cellular phones for communication, the disruption of these circuits would be a major blow to the American animal's ability to respond.

After receiving the flash cards with the specific information, Jason headed towards his favorite morning hangout, the Starbuck's on the corner. In this great city, there was a Starbuck's on nearly every street corner. The cool morning mist from the Pacific Ocean refreshed him. The thing he loved so much about his adopted city was that it reminded him so much of the things he didn't have as a youth. Protected by his family and led to believe there was only a single goal in life--to amass financial wealth, he had learned from his experiences in San Francisco that there was so much more to life and people. The good ones reached out to help people in need. To Jason, his teachings from his nanny Zaki, had taught him it was not the massing of materialistic things was not important. Jason knew buying a homeless person their breakfast, taking time to talk with him to learn he had been forced into this situation when his job was outsourced and uncovering, the fact that the degree in computer engineering that had afforded them a comfortable lifestyle, had been shipped to another country and given to a person working for a third of their compensation, were the intrinsic things others could not or chose not to see in their fellow human being.

Jason thought as he walked, why had America deserted its people? The true Americans, the true Patriots, were those people who awoke every morning, readied their children for school, hugged their spouse goodbye and went to their assigned post to assure the great American economic engine continued to operate.

Unknown to Jason and his team, thousands of miles away in the Port of New Orleans, a ship had just radioed to the harbormaster requesting permission to enter the harbor. Once the harbormaster verified the ship using the computerized database; which showed the ship was carrying olive oil from the Middle East, the ship was informed it could enter the harbor at the next high tide. At this point, the ship's huge underwater doors opened on the ship and six mini-subs and their two-man crews began their thirteen-mile journey to the Port of New Orleans. The global positioning systems on their subs guaranteed each would reach its intended target.

Jason entered the coffee shop and found the usual gang. Missie was a beautiful transplant from the East Coast. She had come here for school but dropped out after her junior year after becoming pregnant. She never went back to school and never went back home. Based on what he knew about her, she had grown up with all of the love of a strong middle--class African American family, but for some reason had disconnected from her family. Her stories of her youth that she shared with her friends depicted love and caring. She told them stories of play dates with her father, night time stories read to her by her mother, and running behind her two older brothers who always hated to hear their father say, "Take your sister with you!" Many times as Missie told her stories about life on the East Coast, Jason thought of his own upbringing. Instead of the warmth and softness expressed by Missie, his parents had been cold and uninterested in him. The only warmth he felt was from the nanny, who had taught him to care for others and yet hate the injustice that many in this country accepted. This is why things needed to change in America, he thought as he ordered his mocha, decaffeinated, of course.

Mashir motioned for Jason to join them at the table. Mashir and Missie had been dating for several months. To an untrained eye, Mashir himself resembled a fair-skinned African American. Jason had known Mashir for five years and they had become close friends. In this city where friendship was essential to one's soul, especially to the souls of those who did not occupy the 71st story corner office, a person's network of friends supported his existence. Friends gave you rides when the bus was not on time. Friends gave you moral support when the system let you down. Friends came along to carry you through the challenges that lay ahead.

Today would be no different from any of the previous days. Jason asked, "Did you guys see those clowns on CNN the other night? They call themselves Presidential candidates. I bet you most of them didn't graduate with a "C" average." Mashir chimed in, "My brother it is no different in my home country. We have people who profess to believe in the teachings of the Koran, use our Holy Book as a means to deceive the true believers and yet they get into office and turn their backs on those who chose them to lead." Jason agreed and told the group, "We are nothing more than ants in an ant hill. Bred to work to bring the goods to the corporate and political elite – Our Queen Ant." Missie was listening intently to the discussion and asked, "Guys what would happen if everyone in America went on strike for a day?" The group continued its discussion. However, Jason's mind wandered to other thoughts—things would soon happen and he knew things would never be the same. Yes, Seif al Din, the Sword of Faith would strike a blow at this county that calls itself home of the free.

Tonight Jason and his team would plant their bounty under the harvest moon. His team scouted their targets for several months. Under the guise of being several friends camping in the desert, they had logged the comings and goings of the power plant's maintenance staff and surmised that the typical maintenance schedule timeframe was three months, unless something broke. This knowledge allowed them to determine the exact point in time to plant their bombs at the sites.

Access to the remote substations was easy. None of the fences surrounding the installations were electrified or monitored by other security measures. The fact that the sites were so remote protected the team from prying eyes. The moon was bright so the team didn't need to use their flashlights. Everything served to secure their presence even further! Their plan, however, just in case someone else was in the desert tonight, Jason had two of his team members using night vision scopes to survey the surrounding area. If someone came close, they would know well before the person was aware of their presence.

Jason thought about how ironic tonight's victory would turn out to be. His team's use of the harvest moon to plant their devices of disruption would indeed be a bountiful harvest for the true believers. Although their harvest would not be fruits and vegetables, the fact that the American would now feel the same fear known for centuries by the Arab, under surveillance and then attack, would be bounty enough his team and him. Mankind for centuries had celebrated the coming of the harvest moon as a time for happiness as it was typical for the final harvest of the year to occur then. The bright moon gave the farmer more time to work his farmland and allowed the farmer and his family and - in some cases in the not-too-distant past - his slaves to harvest the bounty of the land. Jason and his team knew the seeds they were planting when the time was right would produce a bounty greater in their eyes than the pilgrims' harvest in 1620. Although their harvest would not be fruits and meat, the bounty would serve the purpose of feeding the spirits of the disenfranchised in this country run by the elite.

Their car's odometer indicated they had driven five hundred miles during the night. The placement of the bombs and the remote satellite transmitters had gone well. If all went as planned, the destruction of the power substations would occur well before any unsuspecting maintenance worker out on his routine surveying trip could run the chance of discovering their devices. However, the design of the devices made to look like a component of the sub-station's capacitors assured the typical survey worker, who was only intent on checking off the form to show he had actually been at the site, would not easily discover them.

Known as the "Energy Coast of America," the oil refineries here produced well over fifty percent of the gas used on the East Coast of America. The teams riding the mini subs would use the darkness of the night to plant explosive devices that could be activated by satellite phone. Although the incendiary devices were too small to cause much damage, it was not the damage to the oil refineries that they sought; their objective was to attack Americans' outer layer of personal security. With blessings from Allah, they would achieve their goal.

Their ship was set to dock for twelve hours in order to off-load olive oil and catch the next high tide out of port. The mini-sub crews would need to work fast under the cover of darkness to finish their tasks. The devices were attached to the lines used to pump the gasoline from the refinery to the huge storage tanks. The intent of the device was to cause the pipes to rupture and the ensuing firestorm would light the New Orleans skyline for miles.

Once all of the devices were attached, the subs' computerized guidance system would switch on its automated homing device to find the ship. At this point it was a free ride back to the ship as the navigation system took control of the mini-subs' steering. The rendezvous with the mother ship would once again occur off the coast of Louisiana instead of inside the Port of Orleans. This had been planned to eliminate the chance of an arbitrary inspection by some overzealous Port Authority staffer.

Once the subs had accomplished their last task of returning each team member to the mother ship, the subs would be sunk and left to spend eternity in the depths of the Gulf of Mexico.

Chapter 14 - It's a Family Affair

Zachary Carson Wilson awoke to the sound of the television and knew the day had begun. He looked outside and saw it had rained during the night. It had been a short night. As his insomnia had returned and the snoring of his wife had not helped. As he turned towards his wife, he wondered why his three young children were always early to rise on Saturday mornings. He could never understand why they would not rise early on school days, and yet on the day of supposedly family rest, they arose at 7:00 a.m. sharp. His young son appeared at the bedroom door and asked, "Dad, can you cook pancakes?"

Karla stirred beside him. The night before, their friends from down the street had stayed well past midnight. Many Friday nights had been spent with their neighbors discussing the plight of the African-American in this country. They shared many hours of discussion regarding what could be done by those who had the economic resources to help those who did not. The previous night's discussion had centered on investing in the youth of tomorrow, as it was a known fact the African-American community was in decline. How could a race that had gone through so much in less than four hundred years be in such decline?

Having been overtaken by the Hispanic population in number, the African-American community had been relegated once again to having to form bonds with another ethnic group in order to move forward its political and social agendas. The night before, Zachary's neighbor Curtis pondered aloud why his race always missed the boat. Curtis told the group, "Yes, we caught the boat from Africa involuntarily, but we have not since the late 60's when the community was strong and vibrant had the community been able to unite for a cause." Zachary though how sad it was that the gains achieved from the Civil Rights Movement had been lost by his people due to their greed and acceptance of the belief that "I have to get mine before the next guy." Unlike other communities who had come to this country and pooled their resources to generate economic power, the African American never trusted each other. Curtis, said, "Master Slave Owner really screwed up our minds. We don't trust each other and we can't work with each other." Zachary wondered how his rest could have gone through segregation, banded together to fight for integration and used the achievement of integration to create its new reality of separation; a separated black community forged by economics.

The group agreed there were pockets of success where African Americans had formed corporations and partnerships, but those successes had never been strong enough to lift up the community in a way that gave significant growth and security to the masses.

Zachary told Curtis, "Hey, man, don't be so hard on your folks. The white man just hides his failures in the trailer parks and other areas that don't show up on the American radar screen until a tornado hits." Zachary knew this last statement was a result of too much wine and was racial in tone. He really didn't believe the statement anyway. But at the time, the statement fit the discussion.

Both Zachary and Curtis were happy for their families. Their jobs afforded them the opportunity to provide things for their children and spouses, but both of them knew that their overall security was linked to the jobs they held. Curtis was a successful software engineer, but feared for his long-term security as more and more information technology jobs were being outsourced.

Zachary Carson Wilson was a high-ranking military officer with a background that would scare the socks off any hardened prison inmate, but he too knew his career longevity rested on the ability of the country to limit the number of conflicts it fought. Yes, he had killed many men, women, and unfortunately children. The killing of an innocent child had bothered him internally for years. Zachary knew death was an option when he and his men were at war. But the death of a young child? Never fully at ease with this, some relief came with the fact that Zachary's God too had ordered the death as documented in the Bible in Joshua Chapter 6 verse 20, "[20] When the trumpets sounded, the army shouted, and at the sound of the trumpet, when the men gave a loud shout, the wall collapsed; so everyone charged straight in, and they took the city. [21] They devoted the city to the LORD and destroyed with the sword every living thing in it—men and women, young and old, cattle, sheep and donkeys."

Yes, there was a dark side that even his wife and children and definitely his friends did not know. Zachary Carson Wilson was a special person able to turn on equally well the beautiful light of day and the darkness of the night. It was during the night where he issued his country's death warrant to those determined to be enemies. His personality trait of practical expediency allowed him to be highly successful in his military role when he was called upon to handle the most sensitive missions for the United States. Yes, he would kill if it meant the success and security of his men. In matters of death versus life, his only goal was to feed his family, secure their well-being, see them grow to be young adults, and them eventually burying him when that rightful time came. Death was not an option for him now! Yes, this was the dark side of Zachary Carson Wilson, the radical practical side, and not even death wanted to face him.

The next morning, Zachary rolled over in bed and told Karla, "The munchkins are up. I've got to cut grass, take the boys to get their haircuts, and of course cook breakfast." Kidding her, he asked, "Whatever happened to the women of old? They arose at 4:00 a.m., cleaned the house, washed and folded all the clothes, cooked breakfast and made groceries all before ten a.m. on Saturday." Karla, whispered, "They all died!" With that he let out a laugh and jumped from the bed. After cleaning up, he headed downstairs to cook pancakes and sausage for his children.

After breakfast, Zachary called his oldest downstairs. It took several minutes for Zachary Jr. to come down. Zachary's oldest son was much like him although he didn't want to admit it. He could see himself in his son--laid back, not fazed by much, and pretty much taking life as it rolled out. Today, he would teach his son that most important skill – mowing the yard for the continued privilege of living free in your parents' house. Zachary would teach his son how to push the lawn mower, while he himself would ride the John Deere mower his father had given him. Before they could get started, Karla gave Zachary, Sr. and Zachary, Jr. her rules of engagement. They really amounted to only one thing; she told Zachary, "Don't let anything happen to my son."

Zachary was fortunate and lucky to have found someone like Karla. He had always desired a strong-willed and intelligent woman who demanded respect. Anyone of lesser stature would have been walked over and ignored as a result of his drive to succeed in life. A strong-minded woman was what he needed to provide the boundaries to life that protected him from failure. Karla was smart, intelligent, and beastly when aroused.

Karla was Zachary in his daytime phase. She took no prisoners when it came to her family. Karla was Zachary's backbone, but even Karla pushed Zachary hard. Sometimes he wondered why his wife would not just give him a break. Karla pushed hard. She didn't want 99%. She wanted the full 100% every minute, every day, and every month of the year.

Zachary wondered why he, an intelligent, successful man, could not achieve his greatest goal--satisfying his spouse. Only his commitment to the family; his children, allowed him to absorb the stresses placed on him by Karla's demands. He would persevere to provide security for his family and a solid foundation for his children. God had challenged him with his union to Karla. She was a constant barrage of attacks and put downs. Whether he was telling the truth or just not engaging in her crap, it was the same and he wondered why he was too afraid to leave this woman where she was—in her self created septic tank of a life. Like all the challenges he faced, he would meet this challenge and generate the positive outcome necessary to achieve his goal. His children would grow up in a family unit and not fall victim to the disorder of divorce. However, many times now he wondered if divorce would provide the loving environment he wanted for his children albeit the children may have two loving environments rather than one.

Saturdays in the Wilson household were not meant to be a day of rest. After a quick breakfast of pancakes, it was off to football practice for the two older boys. Zachary would attempt to sneak out with his boys to eliminate the need to take his younger daughter who always wanted to travel. He daydreamed often of what type of an adult his daughter would be, given her personality. Outgoing, always wanting to be on the go, and fun-loving--a potentially high maintenance female for some brother, he thought to himself, but one to be treated extremely well if the chosen young man wanted to prevent a late night visit by Zachary, Sr.

It was a beautiful day for football practice. Both of the boys would be enduring their first year of being physically abused by other kids their size. Football was proving to be a good outing for the boys as it gave them the opportunity to spend time outside and engaged rather than inside staring at the TV screen playing video games. Zachary wondered what trend the research studies showed linking the advent of video games and childhood obesity.

Hell, he wondered, if his thoughts about things were true, a hell of a lot of adults must be playing video games, too. It seemed everywhere he turned folks were definitely a little on the heavy side.

Zachary found it hard to give one hundred percent to his family because he knew and felt that people who did not fear death were planning something. Death was the controlling factor for most people, causing them to limit the risks they took in their daily lives. But when a person lost their fear of death, they would do anything in order to achieve their goal. Whether that goal was climbing the highest mountain or diving to the deepest depths of the ocean, if one did not fear death, there was nothing holding them back from tackling even the riskiest of tasks. The latest message coming from inside his country indicated multiple movements of potential targets. The technicians working the computers to analyze the messages were getting better, but the speed of the information they gave him was still not at a level that helped Zachary.

The problem with dealing with an enemy that spoke a language other than English or Spanish was that you never had enough interpreters to decipher the information. The fact was hardly anyone in Homeland Security understood Arabic, and that after that great day in September 2001, no one really trusted anyone of Arabic descent. Lack of trust and not wanting Arabic speakers on the team intensified the problem of trying to determine what the enemy was planning next. What they had uncovered was a major operation underway to attack multiple targets in a single day. The only thing that could be done at this point, until further information was available, was to prepare the highest-ranking targets.

All targets would have their security details increased and other basic systems put in place, but Zachary knew this would not be enough if the enemy was as prepared as his instinct told him they were becoming. He knew it was up to his team to uncover the crack to hell before the fire from within could be unleashed on innocent Americans who had nothing to do with this war.

Football practice ended and Zachary made his rounds to the two football fields to retrieve his sons. After practice, baths, lunch, and completing the "honey do list", Zachary grabbed the kids and headed downtown to the barbershop so he and the boys could get their bi-weekly haircuts. Definitely, Saturday was not a day of rest

at the Wilsons' household.

Chapter 15 – Pick Ups

The rays of sun coming over the horizon from the east were splendid. Missie opened the blinds in the apartment overlooking the old part of the city. In the distance she could see the Transamerica Insurance building. When she was a child, she had  seen this iconic building many times on commercials and advertising material. To see it up close was disappointing because its age showed in its worn exterior. The ravages of time and the salt mist from the Pacific had worn away the exterior of the facility leaving many small holes and giving the building a yellow tinge.

A knock at the door called her away from the window, and she wondered who it could be so early. Probably one of her group's members coming by to get her to go to Starbuck's for coffee. She thought about Mashir -- she hadn't spoken to him for several days, Of course, she was accustomed to his leaving for long periods of time. She never asked for an explanation, neither wanting to push him nor really caring about the answer. Mashir filled a void in her life, and when they were together things were great. But being independent and never really trusting the nice things that life bestowed on her, she never grew to become totally dependent on the love from another human, just in case the love went away. So as it was, if and when Mashir returned, she would shower him with the care and love she had for him. But if he moved on, she would love herself as she always did.

She opened the door to her one-bedroom apartment and was startled to see two men dressed in suits. They both flashed their governmental I.D.'s and asked if they could come in to speak with her. She saw no need to be concerned, as her daily activities had never come close to crossing the line of breaking any laws. She asked the gentlemen to come in and gave them a seat at her kitchen table. As they settled into their seats, one of the men asked her if it was okay if they asked her some questions. The man asked her how long she had lived in the San Francisco area. Missie told them she had left her home several years ago and had fallen in love with the area's openness and freewheeling lifestyle. She said she loved the city and would one day become a serious adult. But now was a time for her to enjoy her youth, before the pressures of adulthood would drive her to seek out a more responsible lifestyle.

The men took this as an opportunity to ask about her acquaintance with Mashir. Missie told them that the two of them had met in one of the local youth hangouts and had become close friends. Both had shared some of the same experiences growing up. Missie told the men she and Mashir's relationship was more casual than anything else. Missie was there for him, and he was there for her when the need arose. The two needed each other more for their mental support than anything sexual. Missie told them that Mashir often left for long periods of time and would always return. She did not ask probing questions as she felt it was not her place. If he was leaving to see some other love interest, it really did not bother her, as it was not love she sought from him.

The men asked how long had he been gone and did she expect him back anytime soon. She replied by telling them his coming and goings were totally random and was something she

really did not bother to track.

Chapter 16 – Tying the Knot

It was a cool autumn Sunday afternoon in the nation's Capital. Youssef was pleased with information delivered to him by Mashir. He also knew that Mashir's usefulness to him was declining, and either he would need to find another replacement for this youngster or run the risk of his frequent visits to his adopted homeland being noticed by the intelligence services of the infidels who knew not of his plans and his place in the terror web.

Mashir told Youssef, "Our planters have completed seeding their gardens of destruction. He continued, "All of the devices had been checked and all were sending their signals to the satellites." Youssef knew the devices would wreak havoc on the country that had turned its back on him. He was smart, he was intelligent and he had worked hard to conform to the western ways on his adopted homeland. Well, he knew now and forever more, America would never be a place he would call home. For a split second, Youssef wondered how Ms. Jones was doing. He truly cared for this woman, as she was the only thing American now that he missed. Yes, the infidels had stolen his promising future, and he would be the one to steal America's might – its Economy.

Zachary began to pour over the mounds of paperwork he had on his desk. His muscles ached from the recent workouts he had taken his team through. He knew it was critical to maintain a sharp edge on his men as they may be called to any hot spot in the world on a moment's notice. The thought crossed his mind that he hoped the hot spot would not be here. He preferred fighting in the wilderness, jungles, deserts and mountains as opposed to his steel and concrete office. At least; he thought, in the wilderness, no phones would rang, no emails to be sent, just you and your men attempting to achieve the goal. And since it was training and not actual combat, you really didn't have to worry about being killed. He loved war games.

Zachary concentrated on the items marked Top Secret. He had mounds of paperwork to go through, but thanks to the military's information screeners, the material had been pre-screened and validated as important by three different analysts. He knew this would be a busier paper-pushing day than usual, so he informed his assistant to hold all of this calls so that he could concentrate of the mounds of data to be reviewed. He truly hated this part of his job. Zachary was a man of action. Reviewing reports and trying to figure out who was the bad guy really wore him down. After a couple of hours of reviewing charts and reports, Zachary saw something that caught his eye. That Mashir fellow had a casual relationship with the Abdul guy he and Richard had overheard talking to his wife at dinner in Los Angeles. Mashir had traveled to Jordan several times. Zachary noted these facts and continued to review the other reports.

He sent his draft review up the ladder to Colonel Macintosh, highlighting Mashir and Abdul's relationship. If they turned out to be nothing more than two Arab friends, then so be it; but that would be determined after careful review of information gathered from multiple sources. Mashir and Abdul had just been tagged as microbes to be analyzed under the microscope of the United States intelligence network.

The big oak tree outside of Zachary's window glowed with majestic wonder. Its vibrant hues of burgundy yellows, and reds were a beautiful sight. This was Zachary's favorite time of the year. The days were no longer humid and the air was fresh and clear. He watched the inhabitants of the base as they went about their daily routines, looking complacent once again. Zachary knew the preparations needed to protect the soft underbelly of his country had indeed fallen far below the expectations of his leaders and himself.

Unlike the oak tree outside his window that had spent the entire spring and summer preparing for the fall and winter, America had foregone its season of preparation and would be laid bare to the ravages of the cold and debilitating winter that some unknown person or persons were planning. In America, people had become accustomed to being protected instead of developing strategies for protecting themselves. Many lessons could be learned from nature, but unfortunately the American President was neither a naturalist nor an intelligent layman.

Zachary believed the military should protect the country when the civilian leadership failed. In most countries, continued ineptness on behalf of the elected leadership would result in revolution, and this had happened in the 1776 in the United States. But today's American was gutless, unwilling to take on challenges that would result in bodily harm. The cancer of complacency had set in many years before and had metastasized throughout the American body politic. People were unwilling to upset the balance of power because they were receiving just enough benefit from the current system to be maintained in a kind of morphine induced haze. Americans would awake in the morning to transit to their jobs, return home at night, complain to their spouses and anyone else willing to listen how bad things were; and yet, they would repeat the pattern the next day.

This pattern would continue for sixty years or until they were told they were no longer needed by the organizations they helped build. When their usefulness was done, they were given a gold watch and asked to clear out their office for some new worker ant to fill their space. Yes, America had become a callous, unloving, unthinking place. Americans had given up foresight the day they stopped studying history in-depth. But history was acting upon their lives nonetheless. Zachary had to protect the zombies, yet he could do so only if he could connect the facts that were flowing to his team ever so slowly.

The dots were many. The death of the Young Palestinian leader and the impact this was having on Israeli/Arab relationships combined with the threats against the homeland were almost too many dots for a coordinated response by the United States and its allies. With the nation reeling from bad decisions made by the current administration, the strength of a Sino/Indian alliance, and Russia's new power supported by newfound oil riches, America was up against the wall.

The American leadership could always count on its old allies, England and Israel, but they too had problems. England's economy had long been in the tank, and Israel was suffering from the fact that it no longer required the protection given to it over the years. Zachary knew these threats required all resources to be allocated to the top priorities in America.

And America had many internal problems--increasing middle class joblessness, escalating fuel costs, racial tensions that were no longer black and white, but had become browner. Yes, America had lit the lighthouse beacon of freedom and those seeking freedom had come. With them they had brought their cultures and their beliefs. Zachary thought, as he reviewed yet another report, that if an American immigrated to Saudi Arabia, he would have to accept the customs of that country; he would have to learn and speak Arabic. However, any Joe could show up on the shores of America, the laws in place require America to offer programs and services to help this new person become successful. What a deal, Zachary thought as he stamped "REVIEWED" on yet another report.

Zachary finished his day by organizing the material into priority piles. He really wanted to know more about the relationship between Mashir and Abdul. A part of him wanted to pick both of the fellows up and interrogate them intensely. However, he knew this was not the American way of doing things, and he would need to wait until the due process system was allowed to work. He packed his briefcase and turned off the light in his office, all the while thinking about what he knew and what he did not know.

The fact that the main Scarlet Badge asset had gone undercover, including Youssef's entire family, was a big red flag. Interviews with the power company and its employees had been done in-depth. Zachary had read the transcripts from all of the close associates of Youssef. The one that struck him was the sad transcript of Ms. Jones. This woman had looked upon Youssef as a son. The idea of his leaving without so much as goodbye, told Zachary that this guy was dirty. If Ms. Jones gave an accurate account of the extent of their relationship, then there was no reason for him to leave as he did, not without a hug and a follow-up call.

Yes, Youssef had something to hide, and he wanted it hidden well. To this point, Youssef had achieved this goal if it were indeed his goal. For instance, Zachary thought maybe the Youssef connection was overblown. Maybe the guy had left the U.S., went overseas, and died. Unfortunately for Zachary and America, this was not the case, as Youssef was alive and well thousands of miles away. Hundreds of years ago, this distance provided a significant safety net for America as its enemies had to sail the mighty seas to arrive on America's home front to exact revenge. But today, America's enemies had only to dial a number in a satellite phone to initiate a countdown on a well-placed bomb. The habits of revenge had changed, and America was ill prepared to respond.

Youssef and Mashir continued their meeting throughout the evening. Mashir had briefed all of the visitors at Youssef's home and thought to himself how proud his father would have been to know he had become so important to a movement aimed at resetting the world's balance of power.

Although Mashir did not know the full scope of the planned attack, he knew-- no he felt with every neuron in his body-- that the planned event had to be large. Mashir told the group, "We must be careful as our adversary, America, would be prowling the waters to seek out threats such as what we have planned. It is good we all do not know the full extent of all of the planned actions as this will allow sufficient cover should one component be discovered by the infidels." Mashir, having lived in America for years, he knew that either by chance or by skill, America would not openly allow an attack and was probably conducting its own counter- espionage activities to uncover any plots. He wondered as he waited for the guests to clear the meeting room in Youssef's house, who his counterpart was on the other end of the table. Who did America have working as hard as he on determining what threats were real and what plans were needed in order to head off any attack? At this point, Mashir smiled widely because he knew in his heart that his American counterpart was too far behind to stop what had been planned even though he was not fully aware of all of the plan's components.

Youssef saw the smile on his young apprentice's face. "You know, don't you? You can feel the energy our plan is gaining," Youssef asked the younger mad.

Youssef and Mashir continued their one-on-one meeting late into the night. Youssef told his young sage, "I am truly proud of you. You have undertaken a major assignment from our great God – Allah." "Your people will remember this day as a day when we brought the great state of Satan to its knees" "I am proud to have known you and look forward to Allah granting us many more days to continue his work." Mashir's relationship had become one of father and son. Mashir truly had inspirations to follow in Youssef's footsteps. The older man stood and beckoned for his young sage to come forward. The two men embraced before heading off to their respective rooms for the evening.

The next day, Mashir would transit by car to Egypt where he would rest and attempt to lose any trackers who may have followed him. From Egypt he would head to Monaco before making the trans-Atlantic trip back to Miami, Florida. From Florida, he would book a non-stop flight back to San Francisco and begin activating the processes given to him by Youssef. As

Youssef headed to his room, he thought how sad and what a waste it would be to end the young man's life so soon, but the trail to him could be uncovered if loose strings were left untied. So at the appointed time, Mashir would enter into martyrdom for the cause Youssef knew was holy in the eyes of Allah. Youssef also knew tomorrow would be a day when he and his family would gather for their daily ride into the countryside. However, the trip tomorrow would begin long before the rays of the sun kissed the ground; he and his family would leave behind all they had known for the past several months because it was time to disappear yet again.

Back in the U.S., unknown to all, Mashir's disappearance and reappearances would no longer occur as he had entered the kingdom of the martyrs several days earlier. Missie would have been pleased to know that Mashir's death had come in a peaceful way. Youssef respected the young man and told his angel of death to make certain that Mashir's death would not be a violent one.

As Zachary headed out of his office, his cell phone rang. The caller ID indicated it was his old friend Richard. "Zachary, I've been conducting an unofficial investigation of the folks you and I observed several months ago. I followed the Abdul guy for several days. I think he's just a father and husband trying to make ends meet for his family."

"However, I don't believe the same can be said for the other guy named Mashir. He moves back and forth too much between L.A. and San Francisco. I've identified several other possible contacts, including some young American kids. The American kids seem to be these new aged radicals who had held demonstrations throughout the country over the past several years." Richard continued his assessment, "Back in the 1960's they would have been referred to as flower children, but this new bunch expresses more aggression towards the establishment. They make the hair on my neck stand." "They are disengaged, truly do not understand the founding principles of our country and would not think twice about attacking the establishment." Zack, "I've run down significant information on Mashir's group and my gut tells me this is a hot spot – one to be watched." "From time to time, Mashir disappears for days on end, only to turn up with his American friends in tow. This group of six does not hold steady jobs and seems to meander through life with little worry."

Richard, "Have you noticed any other activities around the mosque", Zachary asked. "Well the activity has increased significantly over the past several months. Other than that, all seems normal with men coming and going from the Mosque as their religion dictated", Richard concluded. By the way Zachary, "When are you coming back West for another visit" Richard asked. Zachary chuckled, "For pleasure or work?" "If I visit for pleasure, Zack laughed, "It will be when hell freezes over!"

Zachary and Richard both knew something was moving fast underground in America. Like the sewage system that flows without notice until a pump breaks or the system has an impassible clog, the flow of terrorist activity goes unnoticed until death has come.

"Richard, thanks for the information, be very careful as those we are watching may now know we have been watching them!" "You're not officially part of the team assigned to this detail and you know friend there is little officially I can do to protect you." "So watch your ass!" Zachary made sure his friend had his satellite phone number and the number of the team leader in the Los Angeles district. Zachary also gave his friend a key to a locker in the downtown bus terminal. In it Richard would find things that would help repel any attack should one come.

After hanging up, Zachary called the Los Angeles district leader and told him if he received a call from Richard, to treat it as if the call was from Mother Teresa herself, basically; do not hesitate to assist with all force possible. The Los Angeles district tactical leader assured Zachary he would indeed provide this critical assistance. "Of course, I hope we never need to," he closed. The hair on the back of Zachary's neck stood. He knew at his core, that the time was close when his country would call on him to kill yet again!

Chapter 17 - Times Square

Akeem rose early to the noise of traffic. Although his hotel was costing him four hundred dollars per night, being on a lower floor did not provide enough barrier from the noise of the street. Akeem had been in the city for three days. His cover as a tourist allowed him to move freely in this country. However, his real purpose for being in the true capital city of the Infidel was to scout out more targets for the followers of Allah.

He was amazed, truly amazed. Until now, he had not known the true meaning of the American word "zombie." Based on what he knew and understood about the word, the American people were truly zombies. What was thought about American society outside of its borders was nowhere near the truth. Many of Allah's followers, based on information given out after that great day in September 2001, believed that American soil was now untouchable. But what he noted was that the soil could be plowed again.

With the information he would provide, they would plow the soil as though they were planning to revive the great gardens of his homeland. Akeem was fully charged from what he had seen.

Thousands of people mingled at every moment in this place called "Times Square." He could not fully understand why they called it a square. In this deeply dirty place, trash, spilled liquids, the stench of the Infidel, and exhaust fumes from the hundreds of yellow taxes combined to deliver to the nostrils a noxious aroma that would make the pure feel sick to the stomach.

Akeem had seen much during his stay. It was so easy to blend into the masses. Arabs, Jamaicans, Anglos, South Americans, Native Indians and a host of other nationalities all blended to form a mass of humankind that might even hide the great Osama. He chuckled to himself at his little joke!

On his first day in the city, Akeem walked from his hotel to Central Park. It was a beautiful and peaceful place. The thick trees hid many paths and meadows. He took a few minutes to sit on a park bench to watch the Infidels playing softball. They seemed carefree and totally unaware of the danger lurking in their territory.

As he walked farther into Central Park, he noticed people rowing boats on one of the several large ponds. Over the tops of the trees, he could see massive buildings that looked like castles.

He knew instinctively these were the places that housed the city's elite. How would it feel to attack one of those places and strike a blow at the persons who probably financed the election campaign of the Infidels' President? However, Akeem knew his chance would never come, as his purpose had already been determined.

Hundreds of people walked and strolled through this oasis. As he sat on the bench, he watched people strolling by. He could easily tell the elite from the ordinary. They owned small dogs, sometimes several. Some dogs were wearing what looked like clothing. The look on the Infidel woman's face showed her status in life, which was the typical look of distain for anyone who she felt did not belong in her social circle. Well, Akeem knew that the Infidel's wife and children would soon no longer feel safe in their homes.

Not even a cell's nucleus is safe if the right virus attacks. A virus, a small piece of RNA, could infiltrate a cell's outer membrane and trick the cell's nucleus into producing more copies of the virus. At some point, the virus consumes the cell, eventually killing it in the process of producing more viruses. In just this way had his movement attacked the outer membrane of American life.

Akeem noted Peter had arrived on time at the designated meeting place. If they were being watched, it would seem even to the trained eye that this was just a meeting of two young men planning a late morning run. Many people did this in large numbers. Peter was the son of a New York Wall Street executive. During his early years, Peter did not spend much time with his family as a result of being moved from prep school to prep school so his family could secure Peter's position in society. Having failed to live up to the pressures of following in his father's footsteps, he rebelled, and unbeknownst to his family, had joined a radical anti-America group. Peter hated everything his country stood for. The American President was arrogant and did not care about what others thought of his decisions. Either he was stupid or did not have enough intellectual ability to envision the impact his beliefs or policies made on others within the United States and abroad. Peter knew that his role was to counter act these atrocities of this inept person who held the title of POSTUS.

"Akeem, once you enter the main entrance, you will be taken to a staging area where you will be split into tours groups of twenty. Your tour will take approximately one hour. The attendants will not pay attention to the individuals in the group, but will focus more on the inquisitive kid or senior citizen who always ask a question everyone else knows the answer. The last part of the visit you will be taken to the United Nations main meeting hall and you will see what I have told you. Good luck my brother," Peter concluded. The information Peter provided during their run was helpful. After their run the two walked to mid-town and had lunch. The temperature and low humidity made outside dining a pleasure. They set in the middle on Times Square and both marveled at how close they were to achieving the ultimate attack on this great city. After eating lunch, the two acquaintances both went their separate way.

Akeem rose early and headed out on East 42nd St. He walked slowly and took in the sites on his way to the headquarters of the G8 countries. As he walked, he could see the many cultural icons of America: Rockefeller Center, Grand Central Station, The Empire State Building, Broadway, and the TV studios that would carry breaking news of Akeem's fine deeds for all Americans to see. Oh, yes! Akeem knew his legacy would live on for eons in the psyche of the American infidel.

Franklin D. Roosevelt first used the name United Nations in his Declaration of United Nations speech in 1942. At this time twenty-six nations pledged their joint support to pool their resources to continue the struggle against the axis powers. The forerunner of the United Nations was the League of Nations. The League of Nations was very similar to the United Nations and was conceived during the first great World War. As with the United

Nations, the League of Nations had also been established to build international collaboration between multiple nations.

The United Nations building was a simple facility. Rectangular in shape, with a wide front yet narrow base, the building looked like any other high rise in this city of many high rises. Built after the close of the Second World War, it was initially thought that the United Nations would be a place for countries to settle their differences without the need for armed conflict. However, it is the nature of man, like any beast, to find, overtake and kill others as part of his daily routine.

Man has a tendency to think that his supposedly higher level of neurological processing power gives him and him alone the unique ability to rationalize a solution to any problem, including war. Therefore, many believed early on in the United Nations' history this would be the place where the world's intellectuals would come to debate and develop solutions to mankind's problems. Unfortunately, the United Nations was quickly dominated by the intellect of the elite. Billions of dollars, raised by countries with good intent, went instead to the elite of the countries calling themselves the G8 (G for Great). This fact had not escaped Akeem' s leaders.

As he approached the United Nations entrance, he saw quickly that this country was truly, truly ignorant. Had this been his country, one would have gone through multiple security screens well before approaching within one block of the facility. As he entered the compound and approached the security tent, he allowed himself to breathe a sigh of relief. The information Peter provided to him was true. The security screen consisted of no more than passing through an airport metal detector and having bags checked.

Since he had no bags, he would be allowed to pass quickly into the facility. Once inside the building, Akeem noted the building showed its age. It gave one the sense of being in a library. The smell, the furniture, the flow all felt as though one was either in a library or museum. He allowed himself to wander and look at some of the pictures hung throughout the visitors' welcoming area of children, natives from Third World countries, and artifacts no doubt stolen from other faraway cultures. Of course, areas where one could sit and rest while taking in the sights were ample.

As Akeem approached the information desk, he noted two security guards in front of the doors that would open into the bowels of the building. He noted they were carrying only side arms. Truly not enough to repel a group intent on destroying this place, but he knew his method of attack would be subtle. He purchased his ticket and waited for his group to be called. He was in a group of twenty as Peter had described. He wondered if any of these other persons were members of his team. As they moved towards the stairs, his eyes and brain began to catalog the sights. Upon entering the General Assembly room, he saw what he had been told, by Peter!

The General Assembly room was huge. Built to house the elite of the world, it was truly a great room. This was the room where all of the world leaders met to discuss the needs and behaviors of all of the countries of the world, where discussions were held regarding the wars, the death, the destruction and the waste. The United Nations was built in the true Capital of the Infidel – New York City. New York City or, better yet, the United Nations represented the place where the infidel American did not pay its allocated amount to the world and often withheld its amount owed to the United Nations to protest its position of non-support for the decisions made by poorer countries. This was the place where the infidel American made a mockery of the nations that supported the one and only true God – Allah.

As Akeem took his seat, he noted the many white earphones that had fallen beneath the tightly aligned rows of seats. The earphones came from the headsets used by the representatives to hear the translations of discussions that occurred in this room.

Because of the age of the system, the headphones would from time to time detach from the headsets and fall beneath the seats. The diplomat, instead of attempting to retrieve the item would leave it for the night crew to clean up. It was obvious the night crew did not clean up regularly. As he listened to the guide, he adjusted his feet slightly. The adjustment caused the top quarter of his sandals to detach from the bottom of each shoe. No one would notice this as he left the room. The black color of the shoe sole would conceal itself well under the seats. Akeem also smiled intensely as this was the year when the United States' and United Kingdom's highest--ranking diplomats were seated in the far right back of the room due to the agreed--upon rotating systems used to insure all countries would at some point be seated in the front of the room.

America had trained his teams' scientists well. His shoes were designed to carry enough highly enriched anthrax spores to kill thousands. The entire component parts had been designed to escape metal detectors, thus yielding inadequate any metal detecting devices. The predetermined release capsules would break down over the course of the next twenty-four hours, which would be just in time for the next major meeting in this room. As he left the facility, he allowed himself to take a quick glance at the building, knowing it would become an Oasis of Death in a few hours. Akeem thought to himself, this country had spent billions of dollars on homeland security and the only homes protected were the homes of the elite infidels. America was supposedly the land of the free and the home of the brave. However, Akeem knew that only the elite benefited from the freedom.

The next morning the dignitaries began to arrive early. Today would be a busy day. The ongoing genocide in Africa and the newly uncovered mass graves in Bosnia gave the gathering of world leaders an agenda that would keep them at their post for hours. The African representative from Uganda was speaking to the United States' representative before entering the United Nations' General Assembly room. "Mr. Ambassador, the United States' nor any other United Nation developed country has not provided funding to assist the poorer nations in Africa with our need to feed our people and improve services to all regions of the continent." "We know the countries' on the African continent have failed to take full advantage of our rich deposits of minerals and other natural resources." "This failure sir can be attributed to folks who look like you." "Our continent still suffers from the ravages of colonial rule." People of lesser color had conquered their land, become rich, and had left the countries on the continent divided. This division had led people of the same color to attack and murder. These tragedies had been swept under the rug by the international media and the leadership of industrial countries. As the United States representative proceeded to his seat in the back of the General Assembly chamber, the African diplomat thanked him for his time and asked if they could resume their discussion next week.

The Secretary General called the meeting to order. Nation after nation presented their case for moving forward with actions against the persons who allegedly committed various crimes against mankind. The news reporters were astonished that some of the representatives in the council room actually supported a country's leadership even though they were murderers, some on a grand scale. The meeting lasted until 8 p.m. After the meeting, several diplomats decided to visit a nearby restaurant to continue their discussion and also to allow the traffic from the game at Madison Square Garden to clear before driving home.

Several days passed since Akeem's visit to the United Nations building. On the morning of the twelfth day, the American diplomat rose at his usual time of 4:30 a.m. for a morning run. However, this morning he noticed a slight tightness in his chest. He also noted that he felt feverish and slightly nauseated. So he decided to work out at home instead of venturing out on the city's street in his condition. He would visit the United Nations' physician later in the morning to get the normal course of antibiotics and cold remedies for what he thought was the initial stages of a bad New York City cold. Later that morning as he entered the United Nations' clinic, he realized his condition had worsened since he awakened.

He thought it strange that so many unknown faces were at the clinic at this hour. The young receptionist was no longer at her post as usual but was replaced by a young man wearing military clothing. Strange, he thought, as he proceeded to the check-in counter. Then the fear hit him as he instinctively knew today would not be a normal day at the doctor's office. As he drew near the check-in counter, he realized the young man was wearing one of the new bio-terrorism masks he himself had been issued some weeks after the first great attack on this city. Now, he knew, he himself would be a pawn in second great attack on the city. The young man stood, revealing his biohazard suit with oxygen tank at the ready. Yes, today would not be a normal day.

The young man quickly moved toward the diplomat and asked him in a terse voice, "Sir, please follow me to the triage station." "I also need for you to turn off your cell phone and do not make any calls to anyone at this time." "We are trying to determine the cause for the illness and we have been ordered to secure the information flow from this facility." The diplomat was truly afraid and wondered would he see his love ones again. Now he saw other recognizable faces all with the same look of distress. He saw his friend Michael from Romania. As he sat down near Michael he saw the distress on his friend's face. "Michael, have they told you anything? When did you become ill?" Michael turned to his friend and said, "I started feeling badly two days ago. I thought I had come down with a bad cold. But I got sicker and today I thought I would come to the U.N. clinic to get checked out." Michael and the diplomat all had the same thought on their mind – How could we have allowed this to happen again? Today, the diplomat and his peers fully captured the essence of the situation: Something was wrong, and they were squarely in the midst of a major event. All wondered would they come out of it - alive?

The decision was made. There was no choice. The head of the United Nations' administrative detail in consultation with national leaders knew what had to be done. They also knew the decision at hand would send alarm bells throughout the city and cause a major panic. But what had to be done had to be done. The cell phone signal blocking system was turned on and from this point onward only special phones distributed to the U.N. security detail would work. The fact that the UN was now effectively locked down, the UN leadership and security staff knew the news would travel fast. The compound had to be secured; no one would be allowed to leave and only diplomats and their staffs would be allowed to be admitted since those persons would need to be triaged since anyone affiliated with the United Nations could have been exposed to the agent now impacting the health of so many UN delegates. In addition to the security parameters being established, several temporary helicopter landing zones were cordoned off with expectation that the affected individuals would need to be flown to a secured health facility as their condition worsened.

There it was, Ronnie, the father of four noted. The building was non-descript and truly showed its age. It looked much different from the pictures he had seen in the history. Rectangular and narrow in shape, the building was truly a dinosaur when compared to modern structures. As he and his family drew near to the facility, he found it odd that military police were running towards the entrances with what seemed to be military style assault machine guns drawn. The human body is an amazing vessel. Carrying the spirit of a human, which is represented by a 0.5 volt of electricity, the body is quickly capable of recognizing threats, analyzing the threat, and making a split decision about what steps to take in order to preserve the its life. Ronnie wasted no time in grabbing his four children and his wife and pushing them into one of the lobbies in the nearby hotels. From this vantage point, they could see the United Nations compound was being secured from within. Whatever the threat, the threat was from within.

The security details were not attempting to stop people in cars with the diplomatic tags from entering. They were preventing people from exiting. Almost on cue, several black hawk helicopters touched down on the site, and men in biohazard suits disembarked. All televisions in the lobby now had been trained on one of the four major news stations. It was strange to the young father that this situation was not yet reported, but he knew this would change soon. The fact that the military detail was securing the facility to prevent folks from leaving allowed the father's anxiety level to reduce somewhat. He also knew if this was an attack, potentially there would be others around the city. If people were not running and screaming in their attempts to leave the building, then something terrible had happened inside. Whatever it was, it was too risky to allow those inside to leave.

At that point, it hit him – biological agents. If attacks began in other areas of the city, based on the method used, he and his family would not be able to make a quick escape through the Lincoln Tunnel to New Jersey. He had to protect his family at all costs. He also knew bombs were the least of his worry. Nuclear or bio-chemical munitions were of a greater concern. Shit, he thought, why me and why on my vacation? If the threat of death would visit him and his family today, it would also visit anyone who looked like a relative of the perpetrators. Ronnie knew he had to act to secure the safety of his family. His country's leadership had once again failed him and now this failure was threatening his kids. Ronnie knew if he survived and his family was harmed, there would be a price to be paid in full by the politicians who call Washington their home away from home. But the father could not think too much about tomorrow, knowing he had to get his family through today.

The first news van to arrive at the U.N. was from ABC. The news crew established a base across the street from the United Nations. New York Police Department and other national and local news outlets quickly followed. Regular programming was now pre-empted by the events unfolding at the United Nations. The news reporter adjusted her microphone and began stating that unnamed sources had informed her several United Nations' diplomats had been become sick. Many of the ill were being triaged by the United Nations' onsite clinic, but several diplomats had also been admitted to area hospitals. The revelation of this news item hit the United Nations' Security Detail like a bombshell. The U.N. security services made attempts to contact the diplomats, asking them to report to the United Nations for a major Security Council meeting. Unfortunately, some had become too sick to make it in, including the American diplomat.

The reporter continued by stating officials did not think this was an act of terrorism, but were holding open their options. One physician who was trying to make a quick buck off the situation by being the station's talking head, reminded people not to jump to conclusions. He reviewed the multiple instances where people in the past had been stricken by Legionnaires Disease, caused by the growth of bacteria in air conditioning units that did not receive recommended maintenance. All the other stations had gathered their own talking heads in their studios now and were filling the airways with speculation. Although to the untrained eye of the father of four, the conclusion had been drawn and it was time to get out of the city. All that was needed now was a drop of truth and the city would enter into a state of mass hysteria. Was this terrorism or was it not? This was the question now running through the minds of every New Yorker who had survived the September 11, 2001 attack on the city.

Ronnie gathered his family and began moving quickly back towards their hotel located at Times Square and 48th Avenue. He instinctively knew, he had to get out of the city before anything else happened. Ronnie told his wife, "If I am over-reacting, that's ok, as it is better to over react to conserve life than not to react and allow the flicker of life to be blown out by the winds of complacency and inaction." When they arrived at the hotel, he found it strange that the streets were operating normally. People were walking and observing the city's many sights. Ronnie gave the parking pass to the doorman and asked, "Please sir, bring my van to us as fast as possible, I forgot we had scheduled a special tour for the kids today." Although Ronnie knew he was telling a lie, he hoped the doorman would expedite the retrieval of the van as his only schedule was to get out of this city quickly.

Ronnie's wife asked, "Why can't we go to the room to retrieve our luggage?" "Honey, something in my mind is telling this situation is going to go from bad to worse and our best course of action is through the Lincoln Tunnel. If I am wrong, it won't be the first or last time. If I am wrong, we will come back tomorrow to the room since we are not due to check out for two more days."

He saw his van turning the corner. "Come on kids, move quickly, please", Ronnie told his family as he ushered them towards the pickup point. He gave the driver the customary tip, and secured his children in their appropriate seats. He turned his radio on to see what other news could be obtained. "Listen honey", he told his wife, "Even the local stations were being preempted now with the news from the United Nations." He turned onto 42nd Street and headed towards the Lincoln Tunnel, which was only five blocks away, but the traffic would make it at least a twenty-minute drive before they entered the tunnel to New Jersey.

The news stations were not providing any additional specifics about the situation at the United Nations. Multiple sources gave conflicting information regarding the cause of the locked doors at the United Nations. What was known had already been reported. Multiple United Nations representatives had been stricken by flu-like symptoms. Efforts were underway to identify the causative factor, but United Nations experts thought strongly this was a case of poor facility maintenance of the organization's air conditioning units resulting in the unabated growth of the Legionnaire's bacteria.

Ronnie breathed a sigh of relief when they exited the Lincoln Tunnel on the New Jersey side. He told his family to take a look at the New York skyline. Today, they would visit interesting sites in New Jersey and return to their hotel later in the evening to have dinner, if all went well and this was indeed just another instance of poor facility maintenance.

Samples of tissue from the diplomats were sent to the hospital lab to be analyzed. Although a strange disease had struck many dignitaries, no urgency was placed on the need to discover the cause, since the United Nations leadership felt this was indeed a case of faulty maintenance on its air-conditioning system. One United Nations' director even noted this problem was discussed at a recent administrative team meeting as a subject requiring the maintenance manager's attention. Since there was no urgency to review the samples, the tissue samples would not be reviewed by lab staff until Monday morning. It was Saturday. This delay would slow the responses of the multiple agencies that would be expected to handle the coming storm and would allow others to unleash their planned misery on the City in a few hours.

The three associates left the Baltimore Harbor for their two-hour drive north. They had spent a relaxing week in the Baltimore area visiting historical sites such as Fort McHenry, the Reginald Lewis African American Museum, and a few other sites of interest. As they waited for their turn to enter the play currently unveiling itself in America, they did what their training had taught them, to blend in and act like Americans. Up until this point, the stay in Baltimore had been boring, but tonight, they were energized as they knew they too would play an integral role in making sure America knew she could be touched and exploited at any time and at any place. Their goal was not to kill or to maim, but to strike fear into the psychological fabric of this society.

Their target tonight was a manufacturing plant at the base of the Delaware Memorial Bridge. Field operatives had identified this area as a site of opportunity. The target had an electrical sub-station adjacent to the plant. The primary action tonight would be to throw several backpacks filled with high explosives from their vehicle as they crossed the bridge. The goal was to knock out the power to the plant and cause a very large explosion. Since the explosion would occur at night, thousands would see it.

They all hoped their action could occur at the same time as the others, if they were planned. But the true essence of the master plan was that only one person in their network knew the entire plan. This master planner was similar to a bee hive's queen, or more appropriately, since this person gave birth to death and not to life as the queen bee did, this person was more attuned to the first virus that enters a body.

The first virus to attack a human body is able to hide from the body's defense systems as it enters the host, quickly moving into the host's cells and hijacking the cells' reproductive system in order to make more copies of itself. Just when the cell has grown accustomed to its new inhabitant, the virus unleashes its attack on the host. This is the way of the New Millennium Terrorist. The Apex Virus Youssef Aziz, the master planner, had indeed been here in America, had copied himself, and now was unleashing his attack on the American body.

The offspring of the Apex Virus knew they were only pawns in this great game and did not know about the other plots being played out in this great theater, America, on this day. Thousands would see the results of their deed and would not fully understand the potential threat until the authorities had connected the dots.

The Baltimore terror cell talked of the billions supposedly spent on protecting the citizens of this country after that great day in September 2001, but a thorough background analysis proved otherwise. They knew their attack tonight on the power substation at the base of the great metal bridge stretching over the Delaware River would lay waste to the American psyche. The country of America was no more protected than it was prior to the attack on 9/11/01. Yes, more cameras and other high-tech surveillance equipment had been installed at key airports and in the homes of the persons who had become rich from taking advantage of the weak governmental accounting system used to monitor the expenditure of the funds. They all laughed about the one person they had recently read about in the newspapers who went from being a single owner of a non-incorporated company to becoming a millionaire overnight by simply arranging meetings to screen potential airport security staff.

The country's borders with Mexico and Canada were still very open even after the billions of dollars spent to secure them. The only thing that had been secured was the financial futures of the businesses that signed no bid contracts with the government to improve border security. Tariz's entire team had entered the United States several months ago by crossing the Mexican border during the night. Yes, the Minute Men were there, but their numbers, combined with the available border patrol staff, were still too few to cover every mile of the southern U.S. border.

The drive to the Delaware Memorial Bridge was uneventful. The group of three followed the orders given to them: act like Americans, obey all traffic rules and do not rush away from the scene.   The time delay detonators on the three explosive packages assured they would be miles away from the scene before the primary explosion occurred. The fact that their attack would be initiated at night further protected them from discovery. The bridge from which they would launch their attack was a beautiful structure.

Built years before their birth, the bridge crossed the Delaware River at one of its widest points. Thousands of rivets assured the structure would last well past the historical significance of the events unfolding in this country. They only knew the part they would play. Had they known the amount of planning that had gone into actions being played out over the country in just seventy-two hours, they would have stopped to pray aloud to Allah for blessing them and for answering their prayers that the land of the Great Satan, as the followers of Allah perceived it, would be cut down to its knees. The citizens of the United States would now know the fear felt by their people who had suffered for years from the tyranny of the blue-eyed devil.

Chapter 18 – Towards the Target - Movement

On a cold, breezy, damp morning in Washington, the city's inhabitants were beginning to stir. Tariz knew from his observations that car and foot traffic would build to frenzy even on the coldest days in this area of the city, as people of all nationalities gathered to capture a glimpse of the four-year home of the Infidels' leader. He really didn't understand the democratic process but thought as he stood in the cold air that since the majority voted to put the current Infidel leader in office, then surely all Americans hate Islam.

Tariz and his team had been in the city for three weeks, carefully observing the ebbs and flows of the city's residents. He had even taken a stroll to the Lincoln Memorial. Now here was a truly interesting American. Thought of by many as the great emancipator, he freed the slaves only to destroy the economic engine of the American South and its ability to wage war.

As he walked along, he thought that the philosophy of his own leaders would do the same to the American economy. Yes, his leaders had learned much from their Western educations. When the time came to attack the Capitol, he and his team would not be freeing slaves, yet they would have the same destructive impact on the American psyche as this President Lincoln person had on the South.

To kill an individual is to limit the number that can be infected with fear. It was fear, not death, that Americans hated more. With death, one is six feet underground and forgotten about before his spot in bed is cold. This country Tariz believed, did not value individual life but only valued the materialistic things produced by its economy.

Tariz hoped his team would remember their training and the impact the slightest breeze would have on their aim. The wind, combined with nerves, could throw off their aim. All of the missiles had to hit the building. It was not the damage that was important; what was important was to show the American public that they were not safe. If Great Satan's home could be hit, what in this land was safe?

Allah answered their prayers. Robert's stolen van was parked several blocks from the White House; the timer was set to explode the thousand pounds of explosives at precisely seven a.m. Tariz checked his watch, 5, 4, 3, 2, 1. Although he did not hear the explosions, the sirens that followed assured him that the first part of the plan had unfolded. After hearing the sirens of the responding emergency crews Tariz and his team moved quickly to conduct their portion of the attack. He wondered if the infidels' leader was drinking his morning coffee, this clear day or reading his morning security reports. This would be a day to remember.

As Officer Jones drove his patrol route yet again, he noted the usual, including the new guy with his tax-supplied coat. As he turned the corner to patrol the perimeter of the President's house, he noticed something that caused the hair on his neck to stand up. There was not one guy with a tax-supplied coat, but now there were four. And today, the guys did not look like the normal bum on the street. These guys all looked in great physical shape and were all clean-shaven. What had he missed on his many trips through this sector? He decided to drive the block around the White House again to get a better look at the men. As Officer Jones waited for the traffic to clear in front of him so he could make the turn, almost on key, all four men pulled their launchers and rockets from underneath their coats. Like many things, the human brain has difficulty processing multiple inputs during a time of high stress and anxiety. Officer Jones' brain was telling him what he did not want to know. His mind was racing ahead of his ability to react, call this in, no wait, stop the car, call for back up, no this can't be happening! No, what is he reaching for in his coat? Do the other three have the same intent? Stop the car, he thought to himself! They slowly loaded the rockets, aimed, and pulled the trigger. Bystanders heard the sound of the rockets and misunderstood this as escaping air from a dump truck's break system. There was a flash and then a loud boom. All four rockets had hit their target. One of Tariz's team reached for his second rocket and launched it. It too hit its target. Tariz thought briefly, "Success!" In an instant Officer Jones had slowed, unaware of the dump truck loaded with asphalt approaching his patrol car at forty-five miles per hour.

To the dump truck driver, this was just another day in the losing battle of trying to keep the District's roadways passable. He was daydreaming about the evening ahead, while looking down at his cell phone to call one of his friends. He never noticed the patrol car slowing in his direct path. The impact at the instant Office Jones had unbuckled his seat belt caused him to move forward and upward. The impact of his head with the front windshield and finally with the roof of the patrol car resulted in a clear break of his neck and a severance of his spinal cord at the base of the neck. Officer Jones thought, as life slowly left his body, did I really see what I thought I had seen.

Tariz did not see the crash of the dump truck and patrol car but thought it to be a blessing from Allah. The crash would provide his team with further cover combined with the 7 a.m. explosion that had already pulled the attention of the Capitol and District Police from the White House corridor. Now this crash would pull the attention of bystanders away from his team.

The sound of the blast shook the massive building. Instinctively, the security detail moved quickly to secure the leader of the free world. Six of the missiles had hit their target. Two missiles missed the mark and hit adjacent buildings. The President was in shock. "What just happened", he screamed out to the empty room he was in. Quickly surrounded by armed men and being ushered him into the emergency elevator to the secure underground bunker, he could only think about his wife, and his kids who were at school. Were they safe, had they too been targets? He asked questions, but no one responded.

What had he done wrong, how could this happen on his watch? Who were the attackers? All of these questions would be answered in time, but now he had to listen to his protectors. Things were moving too fast for the President to fully comprehend the situation. A few moments later, they were some several hundred feet below the streets of Washington D.C. The President, like any caring father and husband, demanded an assessment of his family's safety. He had two sons in the area's public school system; and his wife today, as he recalled, was visiting a local charity hospital to drum up support for his Healthcare Initiative for the poor.

The current situation was too fluid at the moment to obtain accurate information, but the feeds coming in from above indicated the White House alone was the target and efforts were being made to make contact with the security details responsible for the other members of the First Family. It would not be known for several hours that the White House was not the only target, but that many targets in the country had been hit in a single day. Only later would the true extent of today's events unfold, and it would be on this President's watch, the President who sold out the country with his speeches of security and financial freedom for the masses.

But before 8:00 a.m., it was apparent to the President that his presidency was a failure. As he sat in the corner of his bunker, he allowed himself to reflect. Throughout his life he had used lies, deceit, threats, and murder to secure his position. But he had not worked hard for the status he held and thus did not fully understand the intellect needed to respond to crisis. Having always been surrounded by those who made the decisions for him, today he did not have that network.

Yes, he knew he had taken many shortcuts. His family's wealth allowed him to make up for his personal and intellectual shortcomings as they had influence over powerful people in the United States. But he himself was a failure propped up by subordinates who wanted to see him as a success so they too could benefit from being close to the leader of the free world.

His tenure as President had seen its share of corruption, but he chose not to take action against it. Today, thought, he could see that the folks he depended on for the information needed to make appropriate decisions either had failed him purposely or did not have the intelligence to know what he needed in order to respond to his country's current crisis. His aides realized that their leader did not have the intellectual ability to bring the power of the country to bear on the multiple issues and threats facing the United States, nor did he have the support of the country to make the changes needed to respond effectively. As his subordinates took quick glances at him, he knew they were sizing him up to determine whether the captain of the ship was able to lead them through the storm. If he could not, there were other ships to jump onto.

Several secret service agents had convened an impromptu meeting in the bunker's conference room to debrief each other regarding what had happened. Jim Allen, fifteen years a secret service agent, outlined what he thought had happened, based on the information they were deciphering from the local police and military emergency channels. It seemed the attackers had taken up position on the four corners surrounding the White House and had launched shoulder-fired rockets at the White House. Jim pondered how long the team of attackers had been planning this attack. He knew the security cameras at the White House were trained outward towards areas that could harbor attackers. But someone among the people reviewing the tapes had missed something. That something was very big. As with any attack, an advance team would have been necessary to determine whether the attack on the target was feasible. Jim thought aloud how easy it was to be a terrorist now. With a program as simple as GoogleEarth.com one could dial up clear satellite images of any place on Earth with latitude and longitude readings. The life of a spy or terrorist, especially the intelligence-gathering piece of the equation, had been handed to them on the World Wide Web silver platter.

The first news teams on the scene quickly set up their equipment in order to be the first with the "Breaking News." They really didn't care if the news was correct. In their zest to be first, many news outlets had reduced their level of quality control. Many persons and media companies had been damaged as a result of not verifying the information provided, only to find out later the information was inaccurate. Today would not be one of those days. A blind man could see what had occurred.

The strongest country in the world had been attacked yet again. Not by a flying bomber, or invading army, but once again it had fallen prey to a microorganism, a piece of RNA from a religion where radicals misinterpret the meaning of religion and act on those misunderstandings. At least that is what the spin control establishment within the American governmental system wanted the masses to believe.

The leading cable news company was the first to project this image to the America outside of downtown Washington, D.C. The images were chilling and the story presented by the onsite newswoman chilled further the listeners who were all glued to their televisions and computer monitors. The story of the dead police officer, the exploding delivery truck, and multiple missile attacks on the White House combined with the numerous military personnel now on site led one to the conclusion that America could not truly protect itself. America had been cut, and harmful pathogens had entered the body politics. America had been too slow to close its open wounds, because in its haste to make more money for the rich, America's leadership had turned a blind eye to its open borders with Mexico and Canada. This allowed not only millions of poor immigrants the opportunity to enter the country illegally, but it also allowed in those whose primary objective was not to send money back across the border to starving family members.

The reporter attempted to project a sense of control and calm, but it did not work. It was difficult to provide calm when the White House had come under attack for the first time since the Revolutionary War of 1812. Americans would begin to think, "What had all of the billions spent on Homeland Security actually done?" They would remember the lies that had led to the second Gulf War, the war where the American President had led the country into armed conflict under the false pretense that Iraq had significant stores of weapons of mass destruction. Only later, after six thousand soldier deaths and numerous others maimed for life was it determined that no weapons existed at all. This same President had destroyed the American financial system by implementing failed policies that made his supporters richer and America weaker. America now stood alone in the World, not as a leader but as a bully to be isolated. With this isolation came the vulnerability of not having support from traditional allies willing to share intelligence information and other logistical support.

The damage to the White House was more visible than structural. The White House's construction ensured some protection against shoulder-fired missiles. The damage was not just the fact that the White House had been attacked. The images showed millions of Americans that their country could no longer protect them. America had become a large organism with too many processes to monitor and control successfully – it was too big not to fail.

On the outside, things moved at a high rate of speed. Tariz and his team had exhausted all of their ammunition and now sought to move away from the scene. The Capitol and District police were faced with multiple issues needing its immediate attention. The traffic jams throughout the district caused by a faulty traffic light system that caused all lights to go to red prevented rescue personnel from responding effectively to the crisis. Realizing the situation was quickly moving past a crisis point, the District's police commander made the call to seek military assistance. Although this did not follow protocol, he felt after 9-11, action had to be taken quickly to respond to this situation. The call to the Military Crisis line activated quick response teams at Fort Meade in Maryland and the Marine base located in Quantico, Virginia.

Within minutes five teams of Special Forces units were airborne, heading towards the Nation's Capitol. All air traffic into Reagan International Airport had been diverted to Dulles and Baltimore-Washington airports. All ground traffic had been instructed to return to the terminals at each location. Quick response systems to a terrorist attack were now coming on line. Perimeters were being put in place at set points throughout D.C., allowing police the opportunity to begin the process of checking out people seeking to leave the district. If they were lucky, maybe one of the bastards who took part in this destruction would slip up.

To the most casual observer, it was intuitively obvious what was going on. But for many in the airport's terminal, they just took the sudden changes as delays caused by other factors. Yes, maybe it was a bomb threat or some guy acting out on the plane that caused this recent series of delays. However, the truth would soon be known and the fear of what lay ahead would set in at the airport as in the District itself. Like a virus, the fear now flowing through hundreds of Americans would start its incubation period, then spread.

The reporter finished her report and leaned against the television truck to gather herself. The smothering fires on the White House campus, the disarray of the local response, the look of bewilderment on the soldiers' and policemen's faces told her everything she already knew. America's brain the President and Congress, had no immediate response to this attack. Every American, the cells of this country, was on their own for the near term to determine how best to respond to this new way of life, a new fear of life.

One of Tariz's team members made a fatal decision to run instead of slowly moving away from the scene. Khalid was the youngest of the four. Twenty-one years old and always the follower, he was committed to the faith but had yet to gain the maturity needed to follow orders as stated. So today, instead of walking away from the scene and blending into the surrounding chaos, he sprinted. His brief moment of exhilaration caught the eye of a District Officer responding to the report of a truck crash with a patrol car. Officer Carter, a ten-year veteran of the District Police and former military police having served time in Korea and Germany, thought it strange for a civilian to be running away from all of the activities in play. Hundreds of spectators gathered at the scene of the crash and were definitely gawking at the chunks of debris blown away from the White House's exterior and the black spots that remained from the missile's impact.

Officer Carter followed the individual, and wondering if he could be part of today's happenings. He called for backup and began to pursue Khalid. Khalid was unaware he was being followed. Officer Carter realized he had been joined by another District police officer and quickly moved to close the gap between him and the suspect. Khalid finally noticed the uniformed officer following him, so he ducked into an alley. But, the other officer was waiting there. The force of the nightstick to his stomach was enough to knock the wind out of him, rendering useless any response to his pending encounter with the officers. When the officers finally had him secured, they began questioning why he was attempting to leave the scene of the traffic accident. Being young and immature and not yet knowing the importance of silence, Khalid muttered, "I didn't have anything to do with the explosions." Both officers found this to be odd, since they hadn't mentioned this as the reason for the chase.

They called this in to the District's headquarters. Within minutes, Khalid was enroute to the FBI's office for further questioning. He would not spend the night in jail. If he did not give his handlers the information they wanted, his night would be much worse. Things had changed since 9-11. No longer could a suspected terrorist expect to be read his rights and protected behind closed doors. Interrogation of enemies against the Homeland was nothing short of a near-death experience. Today, Khalid's belief in his religion would be tested to its maximum limit.

Chapter 19 - Lightning Never Strikes the Same Place Twice

A typical evening in Times Square brought thousands of souls out to the theaters, restaurants, or just out to view the sights. Unknown to them was the attack occurring just seven blocks away to the east at the United Nations. People were sick, and the lead security officer, under orders from Washington, was doing all he could do to maintain a tight lid on the story in order to prevent a full-blown panic in the city and eventually the country.

The first people to come down with the symptoms of the flu were now seriously ill. The Army lab at Fort Meade had analyzed samples of their tissue, and those who needed to know knew this was not the result of any naturally occurring pathogen. Someone had deliberately attacked the United Nations and had caused harm to hundreds, maybe by now thousands. The goal now was to determine whether the pathogen was self-limiting, meaning only affecting the host or was it something that could be spread among people through the air. If the latter were the case, they knew they were facing a major crisis, one such as the world had never seen.

The Army scientists had identified the pathogen as a highly developed form of anthrax. They would need to determine quickly through animal studies how the pathogen reacted in a natural environment. On the third day of the animal trials, lab technicians could see the poor dogs were becoming sick. One dog had died overnight and this really caused the hair to stand on Captain Williams' neck. He told his assistant he feared the worst as the outcomes of their studies became more apparent. It did seem the pathogen could be spread through the air, which meant all of the contacts between the United Nations' delegates and staff were at risk. This was the sixth day since the first person from the United Nations reported to the infirmary with symptoms. Captain Williams quickly ran the numbers in his head. Six days, hundreds, maybe thousands of contacts, airplanes, trains and automobiles. They had lost the ability to contain this crisis. There was no way to identify all of the potential carriers of the pathogen. Captain Williams would tell his superiors that Manhattan and all of the surrounding areas would need to be quarantined.

At that critical point, the lights flickered in the clinic. Captain Williams walked from the lab into the corridor to see security personnel running down the hallways. He also noted that the lights had dimmed indicating the facility was running on its backup generators, which could mean only one thing – power had been interrupted to the building. He looked out the window and also noted streetlights were no longer working. A quick glance across the East River showed him the signs on the factories were still lit. However, all lights in mid-town were out. Then the truth hit home with Captain Williams. He knew lightning was striking twice in the same place – and the place was New York City. A new day was beginning, and the dawn was dark.

The attack on the main electric sub-station serving Manhattan Island was really simple. The three-man team surveying this site for several weeks found it strange no one seemed to understand the importance of the installation. Americans had allowed themselves to be lulled to sleep by a sense of invincibility and an ignorance of history. In a way, America was invincible. Yes, invincible to an enemy they could see, feel and confront. That was what made America strong and an adversary to be feared, as their strike-back against an attacker was quick and decisive. Unfortunately, many mighty wooden fortresses in the hey-day of the American Cavalry had fallen victim to the even mightier but unseen termite. Yes, today's terrorists were like termites to the American society.

The bombs used to disrupt the substations were also very simple. One roll of aluminum foil cut into hundreds of tiny strips. The device used to deliver them to the wires of the substation was also simple. This design and use of materials would protect them from threats from any police officer trying to make his traffic quota for the week or some racist cop who thought three Arab men riding together in New York ought to be stopped and searched. Fortunately for them, none of this occurred on their trip to the power substation.

Once there, they watched and found the same pattern as they had each of other times when they had scouted this site. No traffic, just the sea birds and the occasional plane headed to one of the airports in this area. They assembled the delivery devices and shot them towards the high power lines. The aluminum foil's coming in contact with the wires resulted in a feedback of energy that knocked out the transformers, causing the computers monitoring the site to begin shutting down the substations units to prevent further damage.

Typically, this type of loss would be controlled because the system was designed to create alternative routes for electrical power to be delivered to the Island. However, tonight, the Con Edison power grid would suffer many attacks, causing a loss of its system redundancies. Like a human body suffering system failure, a microorganism, a cell of terrorists nimbler and more intelligent than the host had caused the defeat and ultimate failure of the Con Edison electrical grid providing electrical power to Manhattan Island.

For the thousands of blue-faced ghosts living by the glow of their cell phones, this was a strange setting. The streets that glowed during the night as if it were daytime were now as dark as the woods on a moonless night. As they waited for what they thought was a minor inconvenience to be fixed, people wondered how long the outage would last. All train, bus, and taxi service into and out of the city came to a halt. Everyone in this area had been hit by the outage. Why weren't the traffic signals working? Why weren't essential services able to overcome this situation?

No bombs, no planes, no gaseous clouds were rising above the city, so there was no need to panic, and yet, even after the billions of dollars spent on Homeland Security, the city's leaders had not sought enhancements to the city's primary infrastructure to protect them against power outages. Tonight would be a long night for thousands of New Yorkers and countless other visitors to this City that never slept. Yes, this would be a sleepless night.

All of the major television stations had their primary anchor desk here in Times Square. They too were blinded by the darkness, but only for a short period of time. The first back on the air was ABC News. The ABC News reporters had already poured onto the streets of New York. One young reporter looking to build a name for himself was the first to let it slip. He hadn't told senior executives at ABC News, but the young reporter had several friends who worked at the United Nations as visitor chaperones.

One had called him two days ago and told him something strange was occurring at the United Nations. Many of the delegates had become ill, and the administration at the United Nations was attempting to keep a tight lid on things. At this point, armed with the information he had, the young reporter decided he would connect the dots. Blackout and strange illness with attempts to keep the news suppressed were was sufficient dots for him. There it was, on national television for all to hear from a little known reporter that the strange illness at the United Nations was somehow connected to the power outage in Times Square. The executives in the control booth were taken aback by this revelation. Yet, it was too much for them to absorb, because other news wires began to report other power outages throughout the continental United States, and other seemingly unassociated occurrences. Then the big one hit, the White House had been attacked. Lightning had indeed struck twice, but this time the impact zone was much wider than a few blocks in downtown Manhattan. This time the enemy had struck multiple targets including the White House. American's protective systems had been laid bare for the pathogens to pour in and Ronnie the father of four young children and a husband breathed a sigh of relief knowing he had indeed made the right decision to leave the city earlier in the day.

Chapter 20 – The Haul

The inhabitants of New Orleans were awakening to yet another rainy and dreary day. Having survived yet another Mardi Gras celebration, the economically and racially diverse city had seen much during its history. The city's various ethnic groups had lived through numerous hurricanes and none worse than the great Hurricane Katrina in 2005. Due to the inept leadership of the country's leadership, many survived the storm only to return to a city ravished by the flood waters and the attack of the era's new carpet bagger; those individuals who sought to take over the destroyed property of the poor to build another casino or hotel.

New Orleans had become since its post-2005 rebuilding the Las Vegas of the South. Old-style saloons and back-alley "hole in the wall" hang outs had been replaced with glitzy hotels controlled by the elite. Those New Orleanians who made a decent living playing the back alley bars and juke joints had been pushed out by the new investors of the South. As a result, the city had lost its Southern flavor, but this had been the plan even before the Hurricane hit. Many meetings had been held to devise a strategy to remove the low-income residents from Central City and the

Ninth and lower Ninth Wards, so their land could be taken to build a new inner city. The new federal law allowing municipalities to more readily condemn and take over a person's private property was one of those strategies. But the minority leadership of the neighborhoods and city did not support this plan as it brought back painful memories of their history of injustice and disenfranchisement in this country.

The Hurricane only allowed the elite to move their plan forward more quickly, since the city needed revenues to sustain it and to repair the damage. No strategy developed by the Mayor and his team could speed the recovery of the city forward more than legalized gambling and the development of glitzy hotels with their casinos that would draw a regular crowd from the country's growing Southeastern population. So there it was, the poor would be shipped out to outlying areas, including different states under the cover of hurricane recovery, only never to be allowed to call the city home again.

Fifty-three miles from New Orleans on the Mississippi Delta, the sea spray on the boat captain's face was refreshing to him given his late night running the streets of New Orleans long past midnight on Mardi Gras. Captain John Henry Frank was an oddity. He was an African American who owned a fishing vessel on the Mississippi Delta and who lived in a city that lately had not been kind to his race. He longed for a time when he could move his family from New Orleans and move them closer to his boat's mooring on the Delta. Even with the historically bad treatment of his race in this city, he loved New Orleans, a city that had given his family so much. His life was simple and did not generate much stress.

His family in St. Bernard Parrish earned their living from the sea for many generations and the boat he used to fish for shrimp had been in his family for fifty years. She was not a beauty, but this didn't matter. The only thing that did matter was on every trip to sea, he returned with the ship's hull full of shrimp. John was able to provide a nice living for his family. His children had the things they needed, lived in one of the better neighborhoods in the area, and attended good schools. With the change in the makeup of the city since the great hurricane Katrina in late August 2005, New Orleans' infrastructure had improved immensely. The schools benefited from the new tax revenue earned from the gaming industry.   Captain Frank was happy with the changes although from time to time, he longed for the city that smelled of dampness and was dirty even on a clean day. As he boarded his ship, he noticed the first mate was already on board overseeing the loading of ice needed to store the catch in the ship's hull. After loading with ice, the next task was to fill the tanks with fuel to sustain the twin engines for the five-day cruise to and from the shrimp fishing grounds.

His first mate, Harry, was a hard worker. He had been displaced from his career as a musician when Bourbon Street was revitalized to make room for the new hotels and casinos. Harry had been with Captain Frank for three years. The two had met several years earlier and had become good friends. When Harry fell upon hard times, John offered him a job on his boat. The two had grown to anticipate the moves of the others and on a boat in the middle of the Gulf of Mexico, having this trait sometimes meant the difference between life and death.

After topping off the ship with the three hundred gallons of diesel fuel and verifying all systems on the boat were working in accordance with expectations, John signaled Harry to haul in the lines so he could maneuver the ship from the dock. Once out of port, John followed his usual course towards the Gulf's fertile shrimp and fishing grounds. The outbound leg of the trip would take two days and the inbound trip would take slightly longer if they were fortunate to be returning with a full load of shrimp.

The new Global Positioning System he had installed on the boat last week was operating like a charm. Gone were the days when a captain had to know how to navigate by the stars, although it was still critical to maintain one's competency, should the electronics on the ship go on the blink. The two friends began their routines, monitoring the ship's systems and readying the nets for deployment. The nets were strong, made of monofilament fibers. During past trips, the friends had bought up in the nets all kinds of foreign objects dumped there by fishermen and recreational boaters who did not care about the animals who called the ocean home.

The wind was chilly to John's face, but his insulated rain gear protected him from the bone chilling water of sky and sea. He knew this was only a temporary condition as the skies were scheduled to clear and the temperature would rise. The water in this part of the Gulf was amber green. The ship heaved on the

heavy seas as they made their way at fifteen knots to their favorite

fishing grounds.

The sea could be a lonely place, but a quiet place, too. For

a person with a lot weighing on his soul, the sea was also a place

for cleansing. Both John and Harry had used this solitary

confinement to come to grips with demons from their past. On the

open ocean here, both men found their greatest protection from the

temptations laid thick as land mines back on shore. The wind

whipped at the flags on the mast of the ship. It would be another

two days before they reached their designated fishing spot.

John told Harry, "Let test out the new winches we installed

on the ship last week." John knew the key to making a continued

living off of the sea was the ability to catch, retrieve, and return

efficiently to harbor with your load so it could be unloaded quickly

and the ship returned to service. Thus, he had had the ship refitted

with new high horsepower winches that would speed the retrieval

of the nets. With the captain's signal, Harry released the nets.

John and Harry knew this was probably a safe place to drop the

nets and retrieve them without running the risk of damaging the nets on some unknown submerged object due to people dumping unwanted objects several miles further off the coast.

The friends watched the nets quickly enter the dark depths of the ocean. It took a full fifteen minutes for all of the nets to become totally submerged. After a few moments of trawling, John gave Harry the signal to begin winching in the nets. For the first one hundred and fifty feet everything was going as expected, but then they heard a loud moan from the port side winch as it began to strain -it was lifting something heavy? Instinctively, Harry knew to disengage the winch and place it in neutral in order not to damage it. This also allowed Harry and John to assess the situation, as they knew damage to the nets meant a missed opportunity for fishing. Captain Frank felt the muscles in his neck tighten; his trip out to fish could be prematurely ended if they had snared the nets on an object that may have damaged the net. Harry reached the winch and looked at his old friend. Captain Frank told Harry to begin reeling in the net at the lowest speed possible. Whatever it was, it was heavy. Captain Frank grew angry as he knew whatever had ended up in his nets was placed there not by nature, but by another mariner.

As they watched the net slowly return to the light of day

from the depths of the Gulf, they watched also for any damage.

Captain Frank had invested a lot in this net to assure it was as

environmentally safe as possible. The net included escape hatches

for sea turtles and other large animals not intended to be the target

of the net's monofilament fibers. As the bottom of the net neared

the surface, they could see that whatever it was in their net was

yellow. At ten feet from the surface, both Captain Frank and Harry

were able to make out the distinct shape of not one but three

separate yellow-colored objects. Within five feet of the surface,

Captain Frank easily identified his catch.

Ensnarled in his nets were four submarines, each made for

carrying two or three divers. He wondered why someone would

dump what seemed like brand new submarines in the middle of the

ocean. Was the government of his country wasting his tax dollars

again? He had read far too many stories about grants being

awarded to the region's marine biology programs only to be

wasted on unnecessary research that supported documented

evidence on file for years. He was angry, not only because he had

lost sailing time to the fishing grounds, but also because he would have to take the time to remove the subs from his nets without damaging them. Each sub was approximately eight feet in length. Captain Frank could not make out any propellers on the subs, which turned out to be a godsend for him as the propellers would have poised more of a danger to his nets. Harry took it upon himself to climb out onto the extended nets and with steer human strength alone, he slowly untangled the netting from each subs fins. Captain Frank operated the winch and as Harry completed the untangling on each sub, Captain Frank lowered the sub back in the water to allow the sea to provide buoyancy, therefore making Harry's job easier.

Something in the back of his mind told Frank he needed to call this in to the Coast Guard but if he did this now, he would be asked to hold the subs until a Coast Guard ship could be cleared to meet his vessel at this site. He didn't want to waste any more time, nor did he wish to become involved in some bureaucratic investigation. He would mark the spot on his chart. Since the subs had no identifying numbers, he would write down as much information as possible in this log and continue on to his appointed destination. It would be a several days before his ship would return to port with what he hoped was with a bountiful catch of fresh shrimp. Upon his return, he would notify the local authorities regarding his strange catch just a few miles off the coast of Louisiana.

Harry and Captain Frank had discussed many times why someone had not invented an underwater camera system linked to a weight management system that could detect and show objects captured in the net. This would allow the fisherman to expedite the capture and delivery of fresh seafood to the distributors and retailers. Captain Frank had thought of a lot of inventions on his many trips to the Gulf, but he never followed up on his thoughts, as fishing was his love, not mechanical engineering. He set the boat on autopilot system so that he was freed to assist Harry with some of the deck duties.

As he left the pilot house, he noticed a family of bottlenose dolphins dancing off the bow wave created by the boat as it moved through the water at fifteen miles per hour. Captain John Henry Frank loved the open ocean and knew this would be the only job he would ever have or would want. The two friends began what they hoped would be several days of harvesting shrimp. The weather was great and the sea steady. The new winches worked like a charm, and they had overcome the only misfortune, that strange catch they took up shortly after leaving port. Yes, Captain Frank would indeed notify the authorities soon after returning to port. But he would not call it in from sea for fear of being embroiled in an investigation that could shorten his time on the sea doing what he liked best – harvesting shrimp.

Chapter 21 – Uncoating

Several hours after the first news story was reported on the White House attack, Zachary sat in silence, realizing his team had failed. It had failed for numerous reasons, but the major reason was that the American citizenry didn't want to get its hands dirty in the wastewater of espionage. Zachary knew that, those with bad intentions against his country had figured those things out. He hoped the attack on the White House would be the only attack today.

He continued to watch the news feeds on the television in his office when his phone rang. The attack on the White House had triggered the country's terrorist alert system, which prompted a conference call between all of the country's intelligence assets. This call was coordinated by the National Security Agency and included all levels of government. The team would assess the attack and determine the next steps for the country to take.

One step had been taken already; all subway, air travel and public transportation had been shut down in Washington in order to eliminate the chances of the attackers using these as modes of escape. Also, travel in and out of the Washington had been shut down. Military personnel had secured all routes in and out of the city and would begin checking all people attempting to leave the city, at the same time preventing anyone from entering. The interstate highways leading into the city had just become the world's largest parking lot.

As the group was discussing this first attack, news began to trickle in regarding sick people at the United Nations' clinic and New York City hospitals. Based upon early information, the persons impacted were stricken by a respiratory illness. Due to the number of individuals stricken, automatic response systems had been triggered, including the activation of the country's new germ warfare response plan. Zachary knew it would be a matter of time before the analysis from the United Nations would be available. Zachary wondered, could it get any worse than this? At that moment's notice, reports begin to stream in from New Orleans about explosions at the gasoline storage complex in the Port of Orleans.

Meanwhile, the Homeland Security Chief called the crisis line at the White House and alerted the members of Congress to consider invoking the Articles of Law allowing the government to declare Martial Law. This had never been done in the history of this country, but as the military leadership now knew, America was under a coordinated attack from an as-yet unknown source. Things were moving fast, almost too fast. News had come in now about a blackout in Manhattan and an explosion at the Delaware Memorial Bridge.

Zachary sat quietly as he listened and watched the events unfold in front of him and the rest of the team assembled by the National Security Agency. America had been hurt today. The potential number of deaths could not be estimated, as it would be some time before the scientists analyzing the pathogen affecting those at the United Nations would know the true biological impact of the anthrax. The scientists working with the National Security Agency group all noted that if the pathogen was very virulent and dependent on when the affected persons first came in contact with it, hundreds or even thousands could be impacted. If the disease could be passed from human to human, then America and the world could be looking at a major outbreak. The scientists at Fort Meade's lab in Frederick, MD, were working feverishly to assess the threat and they would notify those who needed to know as soon as they had something to report.

The National Security Agency Director summarized for the group what they knew to this point: The White House had come under attack from what seemed to be four attackers using shoulder-mounted, rocket-propelled grenades. D.C. police reported a person of interest in custody who would be turned over to the FBI and military intelligence for questioning. A biological outbreak at the United Nations was affecting hundreds and possibly thousands. Explosions had been reported at the Port of New Orleans and at a plant at the base of the Delaware Memorial Bridge. Early indications from the Port of New Orleans and the Delaware Memorial Bridge incidents suggested industrial accidents, what a coincidence! Manhattan had suffered a blackout. Whether this was linked to the White House attack or just some of the Island's older infrastructure wearing out was not yet clear. Crews were being dispatched, and the power company radio transmissions were being monitored to determine what they found out.

California, Las Vegas, and several other western cities and states had suffered massive blackouts. Similar to the situation in

New York, the power companies had long foregone repairs and replacement of older equipment for the sake of increasing profits. Analysts were working to connect this incident to the attacks in Washington and at the United Nations.

Zachary saw where the National Security Agency Director was heading. As had been the case with anything that occurred negatively in this administration, spin control began early and was sustained by the average American's unwillingness to engage its government in sensible dialogue regarding the direction of the country. So as it was, America had become indeed a colony of ants. Zachary asked, "Sir, do you think the death of the Young Leader of the Palestinian state has any connection to today's events? The Director did not respond to Zachary's question.

Zachary further stated, "Well, we were looking into that. But my team's ability to track the multiple streams of information coming in from the sources the group was tracking prior to today's events had been severely hampered. Resources we need to turn over every stone were reallocated to the crises in the Middle East shortly after the death of the Palestinian leader."

The National Security Agency director added, "This however, is something to run down to determine whether this all is part of what now seems to be a coordinated attack against America. I have been informed that Congress is now considering invoking the Articles of the Constitution allowing the government to declare martial law. Martial law will suspend all civil authority in the country and place the military establishment in control of all of the country's civilian systems, including the courts, police, and legislative wings of government." Zachary, however, knew the National Security Agency civilian leader did not fully understand the rules of martial law. The Constitution of the United States allows the President to invoke martial law with a timely notification to the Congress. It is not a decision Congress controls.

The group moved from the current situation to the future in an attempt to determine the impact of the attacks on America. The nature of all the attacks; except for the United Nations attack, were meant to send a message. The explosions were uniformly carried out against non-human targets. The group discussed the meaning of this at length. Why would someone plan to attack targets where the impact on the people would be minimal? Why? Even the attack on the White House with shoulder-fired missiles had to be understood by the attackers to have only a small chance of killing anyone behind the massive walls and five-inch thick reinforced windows. The other attacks also seemed to be done to draw attention, but attention to what? Was this a plan by the terrorists to draw attention away from a larger attack, somewhere else in the country, or did the terrorists just not understand how to carry out meaningful attacks.

The National Security Agency director showed yet again the ego and arrogance of the current administration by concluding, "If this is the extent of the attacks, then we all should breathe a sigh of relief. Yes, America has been attacked, but the extent of the attack is only some sick diplomats in New York and you know they come a dime a dozen! Hell, it was the United States' - no the President's - unspoken position that the United Nations needed cleaning out anyway."

The data-gathering assets at the National Security Agency were now working at full bore. All analysts and other staff were at their stations and knew the next few days would be extreme as their leaders demanded outcomes that many who had been in the position for years knew instinctively would be hard to deliver if the attackers had been smart in covering their trails. When a virus attacks the human body, the body is not aware of the attack until the virus has entered and initiated its attack. By then the damage is done and requires either an extraordinary response from the body's immune system to repel the viral attack or assistance from the outside, from medicine to minimize the effect.

Zachary Carson Wilson listened intently to the discussions. He knew after going through several of these scenarios only time would afford the group the information they speculated about now. Time would yield the yet-unseen clues. Time would reveal the methods of the attack and, if they were lucky, time would yield the primary cause of today's events. He only hoped for an opportunity to meet the person determined to be the primary agent of the attacks against his country. This would be his target and if he was lucky, after extracting the information needed from this person, he would have the opportunity to place a nice piece of lead into one of the man's cranial nerves.

Zachary daydreamed while the discussions continued around him. The attacks and the fact that his team and others had not uncovered the plots, if it indeed turned out that all of the events were interconnected, reminded him of his college biology classes. He always loved biology because understanding the subject matter came easy to him. The steps of viral replication for instance, in order for a virus to attack and have an impact on a human body, it first went through a process called adsorption, in which, the virus' proteins on its cellular membrane had to attach to the proteins on the surface of the cell being attacked. Zachary thought this was the same process used by thousands of persons entering legally and illegally into the United States daily. Some of these individuals had mal-intent against the United States, just as some viruses had a greater negative impact on the body than others.

Once adsorption had occurred the next step was for the virus to fool the host's cell to allow it through its membrane walls, a process called penetration, like penetrating the open borders of the United States. Those who had attacked the United States today, unknown to Zack's team had entered through the porous Mexican border.

Now the border patrol and immigration services would blame failure on those in Washington who had cut their funding.

Zack knew the blame game was just beginning. He watched the National Security Agency Director promenade around the room as if he was in control of the situation, but Zachary knew none of them were truly in control. They were in the information-gathering phase; and until all of the information came in, allowing them to fully understand the nature of the events, nothing but time controlled their lack of knowledge and they could not act before they knew the facts.

The third phase of viral replication was uncoating and Zachary was truly amazed that he remembered this stuff! During uncoating, the virus' genome or genetic material is released from the virus and is readied for the viral replication, a process called viral genome replication. During replication, the host cell is fooled into making more copies of the virus. This too was the way of the terrorists, wasn't it? They entered a country and made more copies of themselves either by recruiting persons from that country or inviting others like themselves in through the same gateways they themselves had entered.

The next step in a virus' attack on a cell is a process called maturation. During this process the virus and its component parts are readied for release. During the release phase, the host cell is destroyed. Depending on the size and scope of the viral attack and the response of the body's immune system, this attack can have a devastating impact on the body, and in some instances, if left unabated could cause death.

As Zachary concluded his Virology 101 daydream, he knew if his country was indeed up against a terrorist as smart as a virus, the U.S. was in for a long fight. Mankind had not developed systems to destroy viruses, only to abate their effects. And he knew mankind could not inoculate the world against those who had become the noxious free radicals of their religions. Yes, he would hunt down and find the cause of today's attacks and if he were lucky, he would be the one allowed to deliver the death blow. If he were lucky?

Somewhere in the Middle East, a man and his daughter played together in a verdant garden filled with flowers. The child knew no fear as her father; Youssef Aziz had promised to forever protect her from all that was evil. Evil to him was good when the evil was used to advance the lives of persons less fortunate. As he watched his daughter, he thought of the early American settlers who were seen as evildoers by persons living in England, as the new settlers of the New World fought their former leaders for their freedom. The early settlers were also seen as evildoers by the Native American Indians as they encroached on Indian lands and freedoms. Yes, Youssef thought, what he had done, had to be done in order for the world to know that his people deserved what Allah has created for them and what had been stolen by the West and their Israeli puppets. Today the West knows that its strongest member is indeed not strong, but is weak and can be invaded by even the smallest of our elements.

Our plan has worked well, better than I expected. The deaths of the diplomats at the United Nations were needed to reset the clock of that institution that had failed so many. So many in the world need the United Nations to stand up for their rights. Those countries that represent the poor, not by choice, but by birthright, need the United Nations to face up to the developing world's eagerness to take from those less fortunate the things they could not protect.

So as it is, the persons who call themselves world diplomats have to be eliminated. He breathed a sigh of relief as he recalled the reports coming in from the news wires that the attacks on America had yielded No-Deaths of ordinary American citizens. He took this a good sign, as America's public empathy would be needed in the long run to change the policy of their country. However, in the short term, he knew the attacks today would cause fear, as the average American was now fully aware the country they had grown to know and take for granted could no longer protect them. With this stripping away of the truth would also come the realization that each American was on his own to protect his and her family.

The stress and fear of this situation would spread as millions awakened to a new era of fear, not death. This fear would spread across the economic centers of America. It would spread across the Mid-Western breadbasket, the Pacific Northwest, Silicon Valley, and other areas key to the power of the American economic engine. As the people responsible for maintaining and operating the American engine began to feel the fear that now was spreading like a worldwide epidemic, they would begin to think more about self-preservation, thus turning their attention away from those things that had made America work – inventiveness, cooperation, and optimistic drive.

To this end, the Virus; Youssef, knew he had fully penetrated the American protective membrane, and it would be only a matter of time before the American economic engine would falter. America had been hurt and had no protection against this new microscopic attacker. A virus with no cure spreads fear and death. However, the Virus that attacked America would not cause death to people at least not too many people, but would kill the American spirit and its economic engine. So fear, not death, was the ultimate weapon against the economic might of any country. The Virus knew this and knew America was powerless to respond.

The young girl ran through the flowering garden with its running stream. Later in the day, she and her father would visit the market. She loved the market with its many sights and smells. The smell of fresh olives, open watermelons, and apples filled the open air this time of year. With her father by her side, she knew no fear - only love. The sun was high in the summer sky, the breeze blew slightly across her face, and soon it would be time for their walk to the market.

Fear, not death, is the ultimate weapon. With death, there is no cell to carry the fear, because death kills the cell. However with fear, the cell spreads the fear to neighboring cells. The cells impacted by fear stop their normal processes in order to initiate protective systems. As these protective systems are activated, the cell loses its ability to perform its normal duties.

The same thing occurs with humans. If a human is presented with a threatening situation, the human will halt its typical patterns of work, nurturing, and play in order to preserve life. Life adapts to a crisis situation, to constant, extreme stressors. People no longer shop; they no longer visit friends, they no longer work – the processes that make us a great nation stop. When this happens to the American Economy, that great American engine – the economy - is impacted and in extreme cases where fear is rampant, it can be killed.

The young girl and her father enjoyed their walk to the market. She hoped there would be toys and candy from America for sale today.

The end never occurs once the virus mutates.

CPSIA information can be obtained at www.ICGtesting.com
Printed in the USA
LVOW13s1619021013

355124LV00026B/1527/P

9 780615 865836